Maximum Challenge

Joe finally lost his weakened hold, feeling his fingers give way. He slid down the cylinder.

But he had the satisfaction of seeing Rack hit the gloop first.

Then it was Joe's turn to splash into the gooky substance. But he didn't care. He pushed himself up on his knees, grinning. As he remembered the rules for the bout, the first one to hit the gloop was the loser.

Rack heaved himself up. His face and helmet goggles were covered with gloop. He staggered blindly, trying to scrape the stuff off. He cleared away enough so he could see Joe.

Joe could see the insane fury in Rack's eyes.

Fists clenched over his head, R̲a̲c̲k̲ ̲c̲a̲m̲e̲ straight for Joe!

The Hardy Boys Mystery Stories

Available from MINSTREL Books

132

The
HARDY
BOYS®

MAXIMUM
CHALLENGE

FRANKLIN W. DIXON

A
MINSTREL®
BOOK

PUBLISHED BY POCKET BOOKS

New York   London   Toronto   Sydney   Tokyo   Singapore

This book is a work of fiction. Names, characters, places, and incidents are products of the author's imagination or are used fictitiously. Any resemblance to actual events or locales or persons, living or dead, is entirely coincidental.

A MINSTREL PAPERBACK *Original*

A Minstrel Book published by
POCKET BOOKS, a division of Simon & Schuster Inc.
1230 Avenue of the Americas, New York, NY 10020

Copyright © 1995 by Simon & Schuster Inc.

Front cover illustration by Vince Natale

Produced by Mega-Books, Inc.

All rights reserved, including the right to reproduce
this book or portions thereof in any form whatsoever.
For information address Pocket Books, 1230 Avenue
of the Americas, New York, NY 10020

ISBN: 0-671-87216-8

First Minstrel Books printing June 1995

10 9 8 7 6 5 4 3 2 1

THE HARDY BOYS MYSTERY STORIES is a trademark
of Simon & Schuster Inc.

THE HARDY BOYS, A MINSTREL BOOK and colophon
are registered trademarks of Simon & Schuster Inc.

Printed in the U.S.A.

Contents

MAXIMUM CHALLENGE

1 The New Challengers

"Frank, you *murdered* that guy!" Joe Hardy's blue eyes shone as he gave his older brother a high five.

Frank Hardy had just run more than two hundred yards through a fiendish obstacle course and had executed a brisk climb up twelve feet of rope. Struggling to catch his breath, he kept his eyes glued to the scoreboard of the Bayport Arena. If his time was better than that of the last contestant . . .

His lean face broke into a big grin as the numbers flashed. "Yes!" he shouted.

Iola Morton gave Joe a quick kiss, "We're going to be on TV," she cried, her delicate features pink with excitement.

Teammates Callie Shaw, Biff Hooper, and Phil

1

Cohen crowded around, their fists raised in the air. Local news teams pushed their way through the cheering crowd to cover the action.

Teens from all over the New York area swarmed onto the arena floor. In the middle was the killer obstacle course—worse than what recruits usually faced in boot camp. All day, teams had demonstrated their fitness by doing push-ups, pull-ups, weight work, and time trials.

The teams that made it through the morning's elimination round had spent the afternoon scaling walls, swinging hand to hand across rope bridges, and running the obstacle course. They were hoping to prove they were tough and coordinated enough to compete on TV's hottest game show, "Maximum Challenge."

Each week, the show pitted teams of local Challengers against the Champions, a professional group of stunt people. Challengers often wound up falling into some kind of glop. But the few teams who beat the pros won cars, trips, valuable prizes—and lots of glory.

Thanks to Frank's skill in tackling the obstacle course, the newest team of Challengers would be from Bayport. For one whole week, they'd be competing against the Champions before cameras and a live audience. Then the videotape would be edited down to a one-hour show seen on prime-time TV.

2

Joe felt a surge of pride. He was the one who'd assembled the team for the local "Challenge" contestant search, choosing from among his friends.

Biff had been a natural. Tests of strength called for big, strong guys. Phil was a first choice, too. The show often hit contestants with brainteasers, and Phil had the best brain in Bayport. Iola and Callie had good heads on their shoulders and both of them were strong in dance and gymnastics, skills that would be needed in the tests of agility.

A tall, thin man with dark, curly hair pushed through the crowd. His red, white, and blue blazer made him look like a patriotic movie usher in Joe's eyes. But the younger Hardy knew the outfit identified the man as a "Maximum Challenge" staffer. Joe recognized him as Chuck Purvis, the advance man for the show. Purvis had rented the arena and run the contestant search.

Purvis led Joe and his teammates to the center of the arena. As video cameras whirred, the advance man shook Joe's hand. "Congratulations to the Bayport team," he said heartily, directing a big smile toward the newspeople. "I wonder if competing in their hometown for the coming week's competition will get them an edge."

"No way!" bellowed a voice from the crowd.

Joe turned toward the heckler. He saw a tall, thick-bodied man with blond hair and a matching handlebar mustache. The man's hands were jammed into the pockets of a brown raincoat as he elbowed his way to the center of the crowd.

"What a nut," Biff whispered. A frown passed over his big, square face as the troublemaker began talking again.

"These kids think they're hot stuff?" The man in the raincoat gave a hoarse guffaw. "They're a bunch of wimps!" A big, thick hand came out of the raincoat pocket. The guy pointed a mocking finger at the Bayport team.

Joe squinted. All of a sudden, this character looked familiar. He ran a hand through his blond hair as he tried to figure out why.

Iola stepped out of the group to confront the heckler. "I suppose you could do better?" she asked.

He laughed again. "I'll show you what a *pro* can do!"

The cameras zoomed in as the man threw off his raincoat.

Iola gasped.

And Joe knew where he'd seen this guy before.

He just wasn't used to seeing the fellow in a raincoat. Usually, the man wore the scarlet jumpsuit of a "Maximum Challenge" Champion. That's the costume he revealed under his coat.

"It's Rack!" Biff exclaimed. Joe knew the blustering Floyd "Rack" Rackham was Biff's hero.

Joe wondered how different Biff would feel being on the receiving end of Rack's insults.

"I'll show you how a pro moves!" Rack swaggered to the beginning of the obstacle course, followed by the TV cameras. He took off at a dead run, vaulting, swinging, and crawling under the various obstacles at lightning speed. Rack was beating Frank's time when he reached the final rope climb.

Joe noticed a few others in the crowd slipping out of their coats to reveal Champions' uniforms. As Rack began to climb the rope, they formed a knot of red around him, cheering him on. Climbing hand over hand, he called down, "I'm going for the top!"

There was a lot of rope above the twelve-foot mark. Joe figured the ceiling of the arena had to be a good four stories up.

Rack surged upward, past the fifteen-foot mark, past twenty. He was halfway to the ceiling now.

"His hands have to be getting tired," Callie said.

Rack kept climbing, reaching thirty feet.

"He'd better keep that grip," Frank muttered. "A fall from that height could break his neck."

Frank took his gaze from the climber to the rest of the Champions below. There was Rack's partner in crime, Ron "Rune" Gruenwald. He had dark hair and also had a handlebar mustache. Staring upward beside him was Janine Harris, a strong-looking blond girl. Eddie Millen and Stan Dale both had

5

sandy hair, which they wore in short brush-cuts. Finally, there was the team's youngest member, tall, slim, red-haired Kendra Cassidy. Her bright, freckled face registered shock as a cry rang out above.

Frank looked up to see Rack by the ceiling, dangling by one hand. His other hand clutched his throat.

"What's the matter with him?" Frank wondered aloud.

"He's going to fall," someone screamed.

An elbow in the ribs rocked Frank into action. "Get a tarpaulin!" Chuck Purvis pointed to a folded length of canvas on the floor. "Maybe we can break his fall."

The Bayport team members jostled each other, trying to pull up the tarp, only to discover that Purvis was standing on it. They stumbled and fumbled, trying to untangle the length of heavy cloth.

Joe rushed toward the rope and the flailing climber. "Hurry!" he cried to his teammates. It was bad enough that they were acting like chickens with their heads cut off. But now the TV cameras were turning their way.

As he struggled with the tarp, Joe glared at the Champions. Why weren't they coming to help their teammate? Why were they letting Joe and his Bayport friends look like clowns?

Joe led the way, dragging the heavy cloth. As he passed Chuck Purvis, something caught him behind the ankle.

"Whoa!" Joe yelled. He tumbled to the arena floor, dragging the others with him. Joe almost got back to his feet, but Biff Hooper's elbow smacked him in the side of the head, and he was down again.

Gritting his teeth, Joe began scrambling up one more time, when a high-pitched scream cut across the arena. He looked up in horror to see Rack lose his hold. The makeshift safety net was yards from where it might do any good.

But Rack Rackham was hurtling to the ground *now!*

2 Stolen Coins

Joe felt as though he were trapped in a nightmare. He and his friends tried desperately to spread out the tarp to catch the falling Rack. But they seemed to be moving in slow motion.

Then Joe's eyes widened in disbelief. Rack had stopped falling. In fact, he was bouncing upward now, away from the hard floor.

"Suckers!" Rack crowed, his hands thumping against a red leather harness around his chest. It blended perfectly with his uniform. "Before I started climbing, I put on this little safety gizmo here."

Joe's face was burning as he realized what must have happened. The Champions team had clustered around Rack to hide the fact that he was slipping on the harness. It was probably connected to some sort of bungee cord. That's how Rack had taken that fall and bounced back.

The whole "emergency" had been a practical joke on the Bayport Challengers, he realized.

Rack unsnapped the harness to somersault lightly to the ground. He was still laughing at Joe and his embarrassed friends. "You guys need to be a lot quicker than that!" Rack flipped the edge of the fallen tarpaulin with his toe. "Otherwise, these games will be a slaughter."

As Rack turned to pose for the television cameras, Joe fumed. Not only had his team looked like fools, they'd been captured on videotape to appear on the evening news.

The local newspeople seemed to be eating up Rack's speech. "These kids will have to shape up to take on Number One. That's us," he said, slapping his red Champions uniform.

The other members of the "Maximum Challenge" Champions team joined Rack. They began chanting, "Number One! Number One!"

The team that had lost to the Bayport team chimed in. "Number One! NUMBER ONE!"

Joe's hands clenched into furious fists as he turned to his brother. Frank's dark eyes blazed with anger.

Chuck Purvis stepped in front of the cameras,

and the chanting died down. "Well," the advance man said, "we've got a home team—and the beginnings of a grudge match. I'd say this will be one interesting week."

As Purvis went on to explain how to get free tickets for each evening's contest, Frank turned away in disgust, his brown hair still damp with sweat from his run. "Purvis tripped you, you know," he said to Joe.

"But why?" Joe asked in bafflement.

Frank nodded in scorn toward the posing Rack. "The media people love it. 'Maximum Challenge' will get tons of free publicity on the news tonight."

"I'm afraid that's true, guys." Chuck Purvis joined the Bayport team and began to fold the tarp. "You have to remember, this isn't just a game, it's show biz."

"Did you have to make us look *quite* so bad?" Joe demanded.

"Rack's fall is our usual publicity gimmick," Purvis admitted. "And with a hometown team, we figured the local news would eat up the grudge-match angle."

"So you'd get even more air time," Biff Hooper said sourly. He and the other Bayport teammates crowded around.

"It's bad enough you made us wear these awful gym suits." Phil Cohen plucked at the ill-fitting white sweatshirt and pants that hung on his slim

10

frame. "But you made us look like something out of a Three Stooges movie."

Chuck Purvis gave him a big smile. "And now you're the underdogs," he said. "People will be rooting for you to beat the Champions."

"Right, after they finish laughing their heads off at us." Callie glared at Purvis.

Beside her, Iola was glaring equally hard at Joe. All of a sudden, it looked as though Joe's girlfriend wasn't so happy about TV stardom.

"Oh, come on," Purvis said with a chuckle. "We just juiced up the competition a little."

"Who's this 'we' he keeps talking about?" Frank whispered. "Purvis is the one in charge here. *He* set us up."

The camera crews finished with Rack and hurried back to their vans. The losing teams headed for the exits. Purvis beamed as he beckoned to the Champions. "Some folks here think your acting was a little too good," he told Rack. "Let's show them there are no hard feelings over our little bit of public relations."

Rack sauntered by. "Sure," he said, "I feel real sorry . . . wimps."

Snickering, he walked on to pick up his coat. Rune Gruenwald gave his partner a disgusted look. He shook his head, shrugged to the Bayport team, and followed Rack.

"I guess it's not all acting," Joe growled.

11

"Don't take Rack and Rune too seriously," Stan Dale said, joining them. "It's just that they think they're the stars of the show."

"Tell me about it." Eddie Millen, short, squat, and muscular, joined them. "You know, I was the one who was supposed to do the climb. But Rack didn't want to share the spotlight."

"I hate pulling that stuff," Janine Harris said. Taller than Frank and Joe, she looked more like a female basketball player than a stunt person. "One day, somebody in the audience will have a heart attack."

"And catching them off guard with the tarp was too much!" Kendra Cassidy came over and kicked at the canvas. "It's just not fair."

"All's fair in love and war," Purvis quoted, walking away.

Stan Dale rolled his eyes. "And in 'Maximum Challenge,' I guess."

"Competition is one thing," Kendra said. "But we don't have to act like idiots off-camera." She glanced after Rack and Rune. "At least, *most* of us don't."

Frank grinned. "You mean, this is a bad time to ask them for autographs?"

Kendra laughed. "You're Frank Hardy. We came in just in time to see you run the obstacle course. You looked pretty good out there."

Frank smiled. A moment later, they exchanged introductions.

"We wish you guys good luck," Kendra said.

"Just not *too* much good luck," Janine added with a grin.

"I'll be happy to get a costume that fits," Callie grumbled.

"Oh, you'll get that," Janine said. "You're supposed to look like competitors, after all. Hugh Fenner will have that taken care of while the rest of the crew works on the set."

"Hugh Fenner?" Joe said. "We haven't met him yet."

"He's the location director," Stan explained. "He takes over now."

"What about Chuck Purvis?" Iola asked. "I thought he was running the show."

"He runs things till our crew arrives," Eddie Millen said, nodding at a cluster of people heading their way. "Now he'll move on to set up the next contestant search."

"Here come the costume people," Janine said. "They'll measure you and get to work. We'll see you all tomorrow." She suddenly deepened her voice, doing a pretty good impersonation of Rack. "Come ready to rumble."

The Bayporters went to the locker rooms for their measurements. When they got together again to head home, they found that the test course they'd run had been taken down. Crew members in brown coveralls now assembled a huge structure of steel scaffolding against one wall of the arena.

Halfway to the door, Frank stopped so suddenly that Joe bumped into him. "I had a thought on that obstacle course," Frank said. "I mean, I don't watch 'Maximum Challenge' every week . . ."

"I think I hear a 'but' coming," Joe said.

Frank nodded. "But I've never seen any competition like that on the show."

"What do you mean?" asked Biff, a devoted fan. "The grand finale is the race through the obstacle course."

"Those races are a lot tougher and trickier than what we ran today." Frank shook his head.

"This *was* sort of basic," Callie agreed. "There was just enough to make sure we could run, jump, and climb."

"Sort of what we've been doing in gym class," Iola said.

"Do you think that's how the Champions practice?" Frank asked.

Joe stared at his brother. "So, what are you trying to say?"

"Being professional stunt people gives them an edge," Frank said. "We need an edge, too."

"I know what to expect," Biff said. "I've watched the show a lot."

Phil went him one better. "I've got almost every one on tape." He broke off when the others stared at him. "I like to see how they balance the physical and mental challenges," he said, sounding a little embarrassed. "By the way, the last six teams of Challengers have lost against the Champions."

"I'd like to break their winning streak," Frank declared. "And if we know what skills to work on, we'd be better off."

"You can bet that Rack and Rune will know," Iola burst out.

"So how can we get the scoop?" Callie wondered.

At that moment, a brown-clad crew member came by, carrying a huge pile of boxes. He didn't see the forklift backing away from the set. And the forklift operator obviously didn't see him.

"Whoa! Watch it." Joe grabbed the stagehand by the arm of his coveralls. Boxes flew everywhere, and the wiry young man looked ready to deck the younger Hardy.

Then the forklift whizzed by, just inches away.

"Hey, I'm sorry," the worker said. "Thanks, man."

"I'm Joe Hardy," Joe said, "one of the contestants."

"Artie Lake," the young man responded, kneeling to retrieve his boxes.

15

"Will you really get your set ready overnight?" Joe asked.

Artie's thin face lit up in a grin. "Give us enough overtime, and we'll get it done."

"And what will it look like?" Joe said. "What can we expect?"

"You mean for the first contest?" Artie asked. Joe saw conflicting emotions in Artie's eyes. Joe had done the stagehand a favor. Would he get one back?

Artie glanced around. No one was nearby. "If you know a good place to go rock climbing in this burg, that might be an idea."

Armed with this information the Bayport team piled into the Hardys' van and drove along the shore of Barmet Bay. Frank parked by a good section of cliff, and they practiced till nightfall.

Iola was red-faced and puffing as she climbed her last rock. "That's it!" she announced. "It's getting too dark." She gave Joe a look. "If that stagehand was kidding you—"

"We kidnap the guy and throw him off this cliff," Callie said with a groan. "Now I want to go home, have a hot bath, eat, have another hot bath . . ."

"And sleep!" Biff Hooper added.

The Hardys drove their friends home, arriving at their own house just before dinner. Joe didn't have to announce their victory. Aunt Gertrude had seen the early news.

"You kids didn't look very coordinated," she said at the dinner table.

"It was set up that way." Frank spoke quickly, cutting in before Joe. "The idea was to make us look like the underdogs."

"Well, I'd say it worked," Aunt Gertrude teased.

Fenton Hardy smiled at his sons. "This competition sounds like some show. I wish I could be around for the filming."

"I understand they'll be taping all week," Laura Hardy told her husband. "So if you finish that case in Schenectady soon enough—"

"I'm a detective, ma'am, not a fortune-teller," Fenton replied, grinning. Then he shrugged. "I don't know how long it will take to wrap things up, but I'm afraid I'll be gone more than a week."

He smiled from Laura to the boys. "I guess we'll just have to set up the VCR—starting with the report on the late news."

"Tape it for me, too," Joe said, clearing the table. "I'll be hitting the sack early tonight."

Joe didn't know when he woke up. All he knew was that he was thirsty, and his muscles ached. He stepped into the dark hallway and headed downstairs to the kitchen. Some orange juice will go down well, he thought.

No sooner did he open the refrigerator door

17

when he heard a bleating sound. For a second, Joe blinked in sleepy confusion. Had someone set an alarm to catch people getting midnight snacks?

Then he realized it was the telephone.

Joe picked up the receiver. "Hello?"

"Hardy? Is that you?"

Only half awake, Joe said, "One of them."

"Stop fooling around!" the agitated voice cut him off. "This is an emergency. You've got to come right away."

"Come where?" Joe asked in confusion.

"To my house, of course," the voice slowed down a little. "This is Hurd Applegate. I've had a break-in. Someone's stolen my coin collection!"

3 A Sore Winner

Frank had been awakened by the ringing of the telephone. It had stopped before he'd stumbled out of bed. Now he heard Joe's voice. His brother seemed to be trying to get a word in edgewise.

The main bedroom door opened, and Fenton Hardy stormed into the hall. "Who's calling at this hour?" he demanded.

"It's for you, Dad," Joe called from downstairs. "Hurd Applegate."

Muttering, Fenton Hardy went to take the call.

As Joe came up the stairs, Frank was waiting in the hall. "What's up with old Applegate?"

Joe shrugged. "Robbery, it sounds like."

Both boys knew Hurd Applegate. The man had a

19

reputation as Bayport's town eccentric. To Frank, the guy seemed just plain weird. He rarely came out of his mansion, where he kept his coin collection and other valuable items. The Hardys had met him because of previous thefts.

"I guess Hurd doesn't trust the police," Frank said with a grin.

"Well, he won't get much help from Dad. The plane to Schenectady leaves early tomorrow morning."

"*This* morning," Frank corrected. He frowned in thought. "Maybe we should take the case. We managed to nail the last few people who ripped him off."

But even as Frank spoke, the image of Rack Rackham's jeering face rose in his mind.

Joe must have read Frank's mind. "No way, bro. We're saving all our energy to blow away the 'Maximum Challenge' Champions." He rubbed his eyes, then stretched and yawned. "And staying up is just wasting that energy."

The two brothers managed to catch a few more hours' sleep. When his alarm went off, Frank rose, but he somehow didn't feel rested. The feeling kept on as he and Joe headed for school. Once there, Frank was *sure* this was going to be a difficult day.

Guys kept stopping the Hardys in the halls. Obviously, they'd seen the Bayport team in action on the news.

"You and that bunch of clowns think you can take on Rack and Rune?" one senior asked. "They'll slaughter you!"

Some pretended to give advice. "The first thing you've got to do," a junior girl said, "is keep Joe on his feet. You don't have a chance if he keeps on tripping."

Frank did his best to take the teasing with a smile. From what he saw of Joe between classes, his brother was having a harder time. Maybe it was because he was the one who had fallen on TV.

Some people offered their support. In the cafeteria, Chet Morton waved from behind his tray. "I'll be rooting for you tonight," he called.

Frank held back a laugh as he waved back. Chet had better root for them. After all, he was their best friend *and* his sister Iola was a team member.

Somehow they got through school and homework. Then it was time for Frank and Joe to head for the arena. As the van pulled into the lot, Frank was surprised to see a long line of people waiting to get inside. He was glad there was an out-of-the-way stage entrance, guarded by Artie Lake, the stagehand they'd met the day before.

"Your team uniforms are waiting in the locker room," Lake said. "Put 'em on and see the makeup people. Then comes the contestant briefing."

Frank and Joe made their way through the maze of corridors backstage to the boys' locker room.

Their blue Challengers' uniforms were hanging on a clothes rack, tagged with their names.

"At least they fit," Joe said as they suited up. Moments later, Phil and Biff arrived. The four boys left together. Callie and Iola were waiting for them at the entrance to the girls' locker room.

The six Bayporters marched together toward the arena. When they saw the crowded stands, they paused for a moment.

"Wow," was all Iola could say.

They reported to Hugh Fenner, the show's producer. "This is my director, Deborah Kayton," Fenner said.

Deborah Kayton was wearing a headset and microphone over her brown hair. She nodded to the Bayporters, then spoke a few quick words into the built-in mike.

"And I think you know Pat Serrone, our host," Fenner went on.

The clean-cut host was dressed in the red, white, and blue ensemble he wore on TV. Frank noticed the emcee's tan was the result of makeup.

"We'll start taping in a couple of minutes," Serrone explained. "For the first contest, we thought we'd give the ladies a shot." He grinned. "And I hope they're *good* shots."

Shooting? Frank thought. Well, there goes Joe's attempt at getting inside information. We were all set for climbing.

As it turned out, the event involved both climbing and shooting. Overnight, the obstacle course had been dismantled and in its place was an impressive duplicate of a rocky slope.

The cameras began running. Pat Serrone introduced the members of each team by name, then said, "I understand we have a bit of a grudge match here. The Champions pulled a practical joke—"

"And the Challenge chumps fell for it!" Rack crowed.

"Well, perhaps they'll have a chance at revenge," Serrone replied. Then he launched into a description of the first contest.

"Iola and Kendra will have a rock-climbing race." As stagehands gave the two girls safety helmets, Pat turned to the cameras and smiled. "And, to keep things interesting, Callie and Janine will get into the act."

A stagehand stepped out with a pair of odd-looking weapons. They had stocks like rifles, but in place of a barrel, a short, heavy bow took up the front of the contraption.

"A crossbow!" Frank exclaimed from the sidelines. He noticed the weapons were color-coded: red and gold for the Champions and blue and silver for the Challengers.

Callie was a little shaken to be handed a bow. "What are we supposed to do with these?" she asked nervously.

"You'll shoot at the climber from the opposite team. The arrows are guaranteed safe," Pat said with a smile. "They have soft tips soaked with paint. They don't hurt if they hit, but they do leave a mark." He took a dart from a stagehand and touched the tip to his palm. It left a yellow splotch.

"For every hit, a ten-second penalty is added to that climber's time." Pat stepped aside as Iola and Kendra advanced to the rocks. "The shortest time wins."

Iola and Kendra stood at the bottom of the make-believe cliffside. Joe noticed that Kendra was taller than Iola and wondered if that would give her an advantage. Ten feet behind them, stagehands set up tables loaded with paint-arrows.

Pat raised his hand. "On your mark, get set . . . GO!"

Iola and Kendra began scrambling up the clifflike face. Overhead, a pair of electronic clocks began running.

Meanwhile, Callie and Janine set the crossbows and dashed over to the supply of arrows.

"Go, Iola!" Joe whooped.

Frank grinned as he watched. Yesterday's practice session had done some good. Iola pulled into the lead. She scaled from rock to jutting rock like a mountain goat. Janine steadied her crossbow and fired.

The dart caught Iola in the middle of her back.

She cried out, and a big yellow blot appeared on her blue uniform.

At the top of the climbing course, Iola's time shot up by ten seconds, putting Kendra in the lead. Biff groaned loudly.

Callie loaded her crossbow and fired. It was almost as though Kendra knew the dart was coming. She dropped into a cleft between two rocks. The paint splattered on a rock above her head. Kendra had barely lost a second.

Gritting her teeth, Callie snatched up a second dart. This time she didn't aim for Kendra, but targeted the space Kendra would have to pass through. Kendra popped out of her cover, making her move to scale the rock where Callie was aiming.

Callie tightened her finger on the trigger. But Kendra's move was only a fake. She darted forward, then dropped back. Callie's arrow missed its mark by a foot. Kendra got over the dangerous spot while Callie reloaded.

In the meantime, Iola was trying desperately to make up for lost time. But she had to dodge a barrage of darts from Janine. The big blond girl seemed to fire two shots for every one that Callie got off.

Callie, however, didn't try to speed up her rate of fire. Instead, as she grew more familiar with the crossbow, she tried to make every shot count. That tactic paid off when she managed to catch Kendra in the hand as the lanky stuntwoman reached for a hold on one of the rocks.

The Challengers were in a position to catch up. "Yeah!" Phil yelled, pumping his fist.

The only problem was that Iola had to evade a blizzard of paint-bolts spattering around her. She managed to dodge Janine's fire, but she couldn't climb.

A deep voice from the sidelines began yelling.

"Come on, Harris!" Rack Rackham stood in the front of the Champions team, waving his arms. "Nail the kid. They're getting too close. What's the matter with you?"

"It's not enough that they're ahead on points," Frank heard his brother growl. "That gorilla won't be happy unless his team really creams us."

Frank only shook his head. "I guess we see now why they play music during this part of the show. The Champions wouldn't be quite as popular if their fans could hear Rack's colorful commentary."

"I'm surprised Pat Serrone isn't doing something," Joe said.

Frank shrugged. "Rack's annoying a player on his own side. And from the way it sounds, people are pretty used to it."

Then Frank's eyes narrowed. Or *was* that all Rack was doing? As Callie squinted through her sights, her face was tight. Frank knew that look. It was her

26

expression when she wanted to filter something out—something like Rack's heckling from the sidelines.

And was Frank imagining it, or was Callie firing even more slowly now?

Kendra had almost reached the top of the course. Iola was stuck with yards to go. Unless the Challengers got very lucky—or the Champions very sloppy—the first competition was as good as over.

Iola made a desperate break from behind a large boulder. She flung herself from one jutting crag to another. A paint-arrow flew past her ankle, and another nearly splattered on her helmet.

"Show a little life, Harris," Rack screamed. "You gone blind or something? Nail her! Nail her good."

Frank remembered scenes he'd watched on televised versions of "Maximum Challenge." Often, they would show Champions or Challengers cheering their teammates on.

Now I know what they're *really* saying, he thought.

Callie fumbled another arrow into her crossbow. She was so flustered, she picked it up by its painted tip.

Automatically, Frank's eyes went from the splash on Callie's hand to the racing clock. At least there was no penalty for splattering the team's sharpshooter.

Kendra pulled her "fake forward, dodge back" trick again. Callie's shot flew a good foot past her. Then Kendra scrambled up to the finish.

To add insult to injury, Iola was hit as she reached the finish a moment later. According to the clock, she was almost half a minute behind.

The score was official: Champions, one— Challengers, zip.

A triumphant Kendra Cassidy leapt down from rock to rock. Iola crept after her, shoulders sagging. Callie just dumped the exotic blue and silver crossbow on the table that had held her ammunition.

The Bayporters trooped over, trying to make their teammates feel better. It wasn't easy, with the Champions cheering wildly and jumping in the air. In an obviously practiced move, they all leapt together, slapping a group high five.

But Frank noticed that whenever Rack had his back to the camera, his face got ugly. He was still yelling at Janine Harris.

"What a sweetheart," Joe muttered.

When Pat Serrone stepped up to congratulate the winners, Rack grabbed the mike. "Bayport did better than I expected," he blustered. "But I predict right now—we'll sweep them. Shut them out. Rack gives you his Champion guarantee."

Frank realized that every episode of "Maximum Challenge" had this kind of Wrestlemania boasting. Usually, he just tuned it out.

But it was a lot easier to hit the Mute button on his remote control than it was to shut up Rack in person.

"Don't you ever get tired of that?" Frank called over as Rack rejoined his teammates.

The Champion loudmouth turned away from the cameras again. "I never get tired of winning," he taunted.

Then his expression grew uglier still. "And people who get in my way get hurt."

4 From Blanks to Bullets

Joe Hardy glared as Rack swaggered by with his teammates. "What's his problem?"

"He must believe that old sports saying," Frank said.

"Which one?" Biff Hooper wanted to know.

Frank frowned. " 'Nice guys finish last.' "

"And nobody would mistake Rack for a nice guy," Joe agreed.

Kendra Cassidy brought up the tail of the opposing team. She stopped to shake Iola's hand. "That was a good job," she said.

Iola looked down. "Thanks, but it doesn't change the fact that I lost."

"Not counting the penalties, you racked up an

30

excellent time," Kendra said. "One of the all-time Challenger best. I'm sure Pat noticed. He likes to point out things like that in his patter between events. But to be sure, I'll mention it to him."

"Oh," Iola said. "So I did all right on the race—for a Challenger."

"Give yourself a break," Kendra said. "The other Champions have had years of practice. I should know, being the new kid on the team."

Joe half-remembered the news stories about the Champions losing a female member who had had some sort of injury. That's when Kendra must have come aboard, the youngest of the troupe. Joe suddenly realized Kendra was probably only a couple of years older than he was.

The red-haired stuntwoman gave Iola a crooked smile. "You heard Rack ragging on Janine? Just think—she's got more experience than I do."

"It's not fair, you having all that practice!" Callie burst out.

Kendra shrugged. "We're the series regulars— the ones to beat. People don't tune in to see us lose." She grinned. "But when it *does* happen, the viewers love it."

She glanced around the circle of Bayporters. "Just concentrate on winning the next event." She lowered her voice. "It'll be the brainteaser, so get your smart guy on deck." Then Kendra dashed after her teammates.

Workers were now dismantling the minimountain. Hugh Fenner, Deborah Kayton, Chuck Purvis, and Pat Serrone came over. "We've got some time before we put up tomorrow night's set," the director said. "I thought we could take care of some of the filler scenes."

"Filler?" Biff asked.

"You know, the parts of the show where contestants talk about their backgrounds." Kayton held out the cards contestants had filled in. "It's not here on your forms, but I understand two of you have an interesting hobby."

"It didn't strike me until last night." Purvis sounded annoyed with himself. "The newspaper files mentioned a Frank and Joe Hardy, boy detectives."

"That's not exactly the way we'd put it." Joe glanced at his brother.

"And I don't think we'd call it a hobby, either," Frank added.

"Okay, but we'd like you to talk about it with Pat," Kayton said. "Then, Biff"—she looked up at the Hardys' hulking friend—"maybe you could tell Pat about your football trophy."

"What about my science-fair medal?" Phil wanted to know.

"And my all-state gymnastics award?" Callie added.

"You'll all have a chance to talk," Pat assured them with a big smile.

The director and Purvis walked away, and the camera crew began setting up. "I thought Purvis was off for the next recruiting session," Joe said to Pat Serrone.

"He'll be gone in a day or so," the host said. "Hugh Fenner likes a little overlap, so the advance man doesn't leave him with any surprises."

The cameras began rolling. Joe and Frank described a few of their recent cases and talked about the problem of juggling detective work and schoolwork. As promised, the other team members got their chances, too.

Joe stifled a yawn on the drive home. "And we didn't even *do* anything," he complained.

Frank, however, waved him to silence as the van's police scanner squawked to life.

"We've got a B and E at Five-fifty Bayview Drive," the dispatcher barked.

"Did he say a B and E—as in breaking and entering?" Joe asked, now awake.

"And it's on mansion row," Frank added. "The burglar probably had a good score." He glanced at Joe, his mouth opening.

"Don't even suggest it!" Joe burst out. "If we'd won the first competition, maybe I'd consider splitting our efforts. But now, all our attention has to be on 'Maximum Challenge.'"

Joe's fists clenched. "I'm not going to be satisfied until I rub Rack and Rune's faces in the dirt—no, in the gloop!"

Gloop was a "Maximum Challenge" trademark. It was part of the obstacles and booby traps—and losers usually wound up wearing it after the show's mock combats. Fans loved it as cameras zoomed in on defeated contestants dripping with the bright green muck, complete with drippy brown globs.

"How do they make that stuff?" Frank asked.

"You're on the set—go find out," Joe said. "Just no burglary investigations, okay?"

Joe spent a quiet night, avoiding the evening news. He didn't even glance at the morning newspaper the next day, either. But Frank had the radio on in the kitchen. "Estimates of the loss are in excess of a quarter of a million in jewelry, with more—"

With a quick twist of his wrist, Joe turned the radio off.

"Hey!" Frank exclaimed in annoyance. "I was waiting for the weather."

"From the way things are going, we'll probably have snow," Joe said. "I don't want that thing on. No temptations, no distractions."

The problem was, temptations kept coming at him. On the way to school, Joe found a stoplight out of order. Directing traffic was Officer Con Riley. "Well, I'll be. If it isn't Frank and Joe Hardy," he said. "Now, how did you know I was here? I guess you want the details on the big heist on Bayview—"

"Nope," Frank said cheerfully. "We're off to school, then the Bayport Arena. We're steering clear of any mysteries. That's the way Joe wants it."

"Really?" Con looked surprised, then he grinned. "Oh, right, you're taking on that stunt challenge. I saw you on TV." He clearly enjoyed the memory of Joe falling on his face.

Joe gritted his teeth. But all he said was, "Aren't we blocking traffic, Con?"

At last, the Hardys reached school. Joe went from homeroom to homeroom, distributing tickets for the evening's competition.

"Wow!" A junior girl snatched tickets from his hand. "We'll see Rack and Rune in person."

"I love Rack," one girl said. "He's so hot."

"Rune is such a hunk," another girl said with a sigh.

"I don't know about Rune," Joe growled. "But I know Rack is a total jerk."

As Joe left the classroom, one of Iola's friends stopped him. "It's a shame about what happened last night. We were really rooting for you guys." She shook her head. "Iola did so well at first."

Joe nodded. "We have a new chance tonight."

The girl looked eager. "Do you know what this evening's match will be?"

"Not exactly," Joe admitted. "But we think it's brain-busting time. And we'll have Phil Cohen on the line."

The streets around the arena were jammed as the Hardys arrived that evening. "The crowd is even bigger than last night," Frank said. "Pat Serrone was on 'Sports View' last night, talking up Iola's effort. Maybe Purvis was right about this underdog thing."

"Let's hope the crowd roots for us." Joe pulled up by the stage door. A familiar, wiry, brown-clad figure stood guard just inside the door. It was Artie Lake, the stagehand who'd befriended them.

"Hey, the boy detectives." Artie greeted them with a teasing grin.

"That's us," Frank joshed back. "We'd have been in earlier, but the cops want us to stop a crime wave. Two big burglaries in two days."

"Yeah." Joe joined in on the joke. "The town's not safe since your crew arrived. Guess us boy detectives will have to start stirring things up around here."

Artie's grin faded. "What do you mean?"

"Grilling people, background checks—" Joe put

on his best tough-cop voice. "For instance, where were *you* last night around eleven o'clock?"

For a second, panic showed in Artie's eyes. Then his thin face flushed with anger. "Maybe you think provoking people is funny. But I don't."

A knot of production people—Hugh Fenner, Deborah Kayton, and Chuck Purvis—glanced over as the conversation got louder.

"Hey, Artie," Frank said, hoping to calm things down. "Show people always got blamed for crimes in the old days. People would lock up their silver when actors came to town—right, Mr. Fenner?"

The producer nodded, smiling. "You know your history, Frank. Landladies wouldn't even rent rooms to theater types."

"I wonder where Rack and Rune would have been then," Joe said, grinning.

But Frank wasn't smiling as the brothers headed for the locker room. "I think you pushed too hard with Artie," he said quietly. "We may regret that if we want more information from him."

"I think he recovered," Joe responded. "We can't worry about it now, though. We've got to concentrate on the next game." They joined their teammates after silently donning their uniforms.

"At least they got the paint out." Iola twisted to look at her back. "I was afraid people would start calling me 'Spot.'"

"Let's get this show on the road," Joe said.

But as they headed for the arena floor, they found several stagehands blocking the way.

"Sorry," one of the crew members said. "You can't come out yet."

"Why not?" Frank said in annoyance. "Is Rack making another speech?"

A short guy who usually handled props shook his head. "They don't want you to see—"

His coworker poked him. "Quiet, Harry!"

The Bayporters stepped back. "I think this will be a challenge for brains rather than brawn," Phil Cohen spoke up. "Those usually involve mazes with built-in puzzles. That's why they don't want to give us an advance look."

"Hmm," Frank said. "The prop guy is one of the people keeping us out of the arena. I wonder what the prop table might tell us?"

They strolled away, trying to look casual. But the prop table held no clues.

"Empty!" Iola said in disgust, turning away.

Just then, Artie Lake rushed up, carrying a box. He plunked it on the table and dashed off.

Looks like he got a promotion, Joe thought. From door guard to stand-in prop man.

Iola immediately took a peek inside the box. "Whoa," she exclaimed. She pulled a pistol out of the box.

"Is it real?" Callie asked.

"It's heavy." Iola held the gun in two hands.

"Definitely brain-teasing time," Phil said. "I wonder if they shoot into the air to distract contestants."

Biff peered at the gun. "Why not use a starter's pistol, instead of the real thing?"

"Beats me," Frank said. "Even loaded with blanks, a real gun can be dangerous."

"Well, I know some people I'd like to use this on." Iola waved the pistol in her two hands. "Where's that Rack guy? Or Janine and Kendra?"

"Hey!" Phil ducked as the gun pointed at him.

"Back off," Iola mock-threatened, taking aim.

"*Iola!*" Frank stepped forward.

Joe gently took hold of Iola's wrists, aiming the gun up. Then he took it away from her.

"That's not a toy," Frank scolded.

"Lighten up," Iola pouted. "The dumb thing is loaded with blanks."

"Well, I'm going to unload it and put it back in the box." Joe popped open the cylinder and shook the bullets out. "I'll just leave these inside the trigger guard—"

He suddenly broke off.

"What's the matter?" Iola asked.

"Six bullets," Joe said quietly.

"That's stupid." Frank frowned. "For safety, revolvers usually have one cylinder empty."

"That may have been how this gun started out." Joe held out his hand. "Then somebody stuck in another bullet." He met Frank's eyes.

"A real one."

5 Thief in the Night

Frank saw Iola turn white. "Th-there's a real bullet in there?" She gulped. "Well, at least the safety was on."

"Iola," Joe said gently, "revolvers don't have safeties."

Iola's knees suddenly buckled. Luckily, Frank was close enough to grab her. "I'm glad you're not the one competing tonight," he said.

Biff laughed. "I don't think Phil is taking it too well, either."

Frank had to admit that their top brain looked a little pale. Of course, he thought, looking down the barrel of a loaded gun usually has that effect.

But Frank had other concerns. "What I'd like to know is where the bullet came from."

"Accidents happen," Joe said. "There was a movie recently where a live round wound up in a gun. The star got killed."

Phil finally spoke. "That makes me feel *so* much better."

Joe put the gun back in the box, leaving the five blank rounds resting on the trigger guard. As he did that, Chuck Purvis came over. "I hope you're not fooling with our prop gun," he said. "Even blanks can be dangerous."

"It's even more dangerous to find this under the hammer." Joe tossed over the real bullet.

Purvis's reaction was immediate. "This was actually in the gun?" he said angrily. "I'm going to take this up with Fenner."

He scooped up the box, pistol and all, and stalked off.

Joe's eyebrows went up. "Well," he muttered, "at least we've improved the show's safety."

"But we still don't know who left that bullet," Frank replied.

"I don't think it's much of a mystery," Joe said. "We only have to look around for someone who wants to psych us out. That makes the answer pretty obvious. Rack did it."

"If this is supposed to be psychological warfare, it's not a very smart move." Frank frowned. "How were we supposed to know there was a real bullet in the gun? Pat Serrone would be firing the thing into the air."

"Nobody ever suggested Rack was a genius," Joe said. Then his eyes got big. "What if the bullet had hit someone?"

"It nearly happened with Phil," Frank pointed out. "But somehow, setting up an accidental shooting doesn't strike me as Rack's style."

"A punch in the face would be more his style," Joe admitted. "But who else would have done this?"

"I've got a candidate, although I don't like to say it," Frank said. "Artie Lake."

"What?" Joe stared in disbelief.

"Who stuck the gun under our noses in the first place? Artie's not the prop guy. He's a low-level grunt on the production crew." Frank frowned. "He also got bent out of shape when you suggested a connection between the break-ins and the show's arrival. Suppose, just for a second, you were right and that Artie or another crew member is actually the burglar?"

"And he took us seriously about investigating the show's staff?" Joe's face twisted in thought. "If I were Artie, I'd arrange for an accident on the set, rather than a long shot like this." He rolled his eyes. "If you'll pardon the expression."

Frank smiled faintly. "Very funny. But seriously,

43

if he wanted to get rid of us, there are easier ways than a shooting mishap."

"Especially since there was only one bullet for two boy detectives," Joe added with a grin.

Frank's eyes got a faraway look. "Of course, it could have been a warning. But that would depend on our finding the bullet."

"As you said, Artie plunked the gun down in front of us," Joe pointed out. "Maybe he figured our curiosity would take care of the rest."

"That would make sense if he'd done something —anything—to get us to look at the gun." Frank threw up his hands in frustration. "But he didn't. It just doesn't add up."

Joe shrugged. "Unless it was truly an accident."

"Which is where we started." Frustrated, Frank set off after Chuck Purvis. The show's advance man had been stopped by a crew member. As they talked, Purvis held the box as if it were a bomb. When Frank caught up to him a deep frown creased Purvis's face.

"I decided to come along with you to talk to Mr. Fenner," Frank said.

Purvis looked a little upset. "To complain?"

"To explain," Frank replied. He spotted the producer and director. "Let's go."

Fenner and Kayton were horrified to hear Purvis's report. "I've run this show for nearly five years," Fenner said. "And I've never seen a safety violation like this."

"Not even as a prank?" Frank asked.

"Never," Fenner answered. "Anyone who would pull a stunt like that would be dropped from the show."

That would eliminate Rack from the list of suspects, Frank thought. But there was still the possible burglar. "The box with the gun was left by Artie Lake," Frank said. "What do you know about him?"

Deborah Kayton shrugged. "He's an assistant rigger and gofer. What do we need to know about a guy who moves boxes around?"

"As you just heard, Joe and I had a run-in with Artie at the door," Frank said. "He got pretty worked up when Joe suggested a link between some local burglaries and the arrival of the crew."

"Artie? A burglar?" Purvis said. "Maybe we should keep an eye on him."

"Great advice, considering you'll be in Boston tomorrow." Kayton frowned. "I'll call our head office and get his employment form."

"I don't suppose you and your brother would want to look into this," Fenner said.

Joe will kill me if I say yes, Frank thought. "We can investigate, or we can compete. We can't do both. I just thought you should be aware—in case the police start asking questions."

Frank headed back to his teammates. The reception committee that had barred the door now came toward them. "You're on," a crew member said.

Harry, the regular prop man, glanced at the table. "Hey! There's supposed to be a gun here." He gave the Bayporters a suspicious look. "You guys didn't—"

"Go see Mr. Fenner," Frank advised as he and his teammates marched off.

The arena floor had been transformed into a three-dimensional maze. A structure of steel pipes rose stiltlike from a sea of gloop, supporting plywood platforms of different heights. The tallest island stood thirty feet high, the lowest was a bare five feet above the gloop. Some islands were connected by a strand of cable stretched like a tightrope. For others, planks served as bridges from platform to platform. To get to some islets, contestants would have to swing Tarzan-style.

In the middle of the arena rose a medium-high island with a white flag.

"This is our problem-solving challenge," Pat Serrone said. "Who will represent your team?"

"I will," Phil said.

"Okay. The aim of this game is for you to make it to the safety of the island with the white flag. Until you reach the safe island, you'll be pursued by two opponents."

Pat nodded toward Rune and Stan Dale. The host turned to a brown-suited costume person, who put a headband around Phil's forehead. Three large feathers jutted over the band.

"These feathers are your three lives," Serrone said. "Don't let the pursuers grab them. Lose all three feathers and you lose the event."

Pat led Phil to the entrance of the island-maze. "We'll give you a ten-second lead on your pursuers," Pat said. "Starting . . . *now!*"

Phil dashed to the first island. It led to two others, one over a plank bridge, and one by a rope strung at head-height. Phil dashed over the bridge. The new island had a swinging rope to a lower island, which had a plank bridge leading to yet another platform.

As his teammates cheered Phil on, Joe turned to Frank. "It's easy to swing *down*. But what happens if he has to swing up?"

Phil's head start ran out, and Rune and Stan thundered into the maze. The two Champions immediately split up.

Frank began to realize there was more to this race than simple running. Positions counted, too. Stan could move to one island and cut off half the maze while Rune tracked Phil down.

But it seemed as though Phil had figured that out already. He climbed hand over hand to a rope bridge, then scrambled up scaffolding to a high island. He stood there a moment, peering toward the white-flagged islet.

Joe cheered. "He's scouting a route!"

"But he can't stay there too long," Frank said. "Those lugs will be coming after him from two directions."

As if he'd heard Frank's warning, Phil moved. But he headed *away* from the safe zone.

"What's he doing?" Biff asked.

Frank could only shrug in puzzlement.

Phil seemed headed on a collision course with Stan Dale. The Champion stuntman seemed as baffled as Frank.

Phil and Stan were heading for the same island. Phil put on a burst of speed, beating Stan. But the stuntman arrived a second after. His hand went out to snatch a feather from Phil's headband. He got it!

At the same moment, Phil swung away on a rope. Stan went to pursue—and couldn't. He had no way of getting to the island Phil had just reached. And Phil tied the swinging rope in place on his side of the gloop.

"Good move," Frank said. "He paid one life to outsmart Stan." The stuntman would have to re-trace half his route to come after Phil again.

"Yeah," Iola cried, "But here comes Rune."

The other Champion charged ahead to catch Phil. But the Bayport Challenger wasn't standing still. He headed for another island, a four-way connection.

Phil dropped to one knee at a plank bridge leading off his island. Rune swung in to land with a crash on the island next to it.

"We're about to lose another feather," Joe said unhappily.

Then Phil rose—with the plank clutched in his hands, leaving Rune teetering on the edge of his platform. The bridge he'd planned to charge across had just been yanked away. Phil swung the plank onto his shoulder and set off across another bridge.

In the stands, the Bayport crowd went crazy.

Rack burst from the ranks of the Champions. Screaming, he stormed over to Pat Serrone, who simply shook his head.

"Go, Phil!" Joe yelled. "That's a good trick. But why is he carrying that board?"

Frank stared hard at the island of safety. He'd been so busy looking at the white flag, he'd missed something. But Phil hadn't.

"There are no bridges to the safe zone," Frank said. "So Phil pulled a double move. First, he faked those two out of position. And while he was doing that, he picked up the longest plank to make himself a bridge."

Now Rune had to backtrack. But Stan was coming up quickly. Phil dashed for the safe zone just as Stan managed to reach a blocking position.

He skidded to a halt when he saw Stan. The Champion stood on the island closest to the safety zone. The next-closest island had a swinging rope —on the opposite side. To get there, Phil would have to traverse half the maze. And Rune was beginning to close in.

Phil took a gamble. He swung across, holding his plank like a lance.

"Phil's trying to run past Stan!" Callie cried.

Phil's plan almost worked. Stan had to step aside to avoid the plank, but he managed to snatch a feather as Phil passed. And when Phil lunged with the plank to bridge the gap, the plank came up short. He swung off the island, leaving his plank half-off, half-on the platform.

"Two down." The dull tone of defeat filled Iola's voice. "We've had it."

Frank frowned, thinking quickly. That plank was the longest in the maze. If it couldn't reach the safe zone, how could Phil make it?

Apparently, Phil had an idea. He raced from island to island, seeming to aim for Rune. Behind him, Stan was in full pursuit. The Champions obviously had a plan to catch Phil between them.

Phil knelt to grab another plank—a much shorter one.

"What's he doing now?" Biff demanded. Rune arrived at the island across the way. He halted for a second, measuring the gap. Then he tried a long jump to catch Phil.

He was inches short, just missing the edge of the island. As he dropped into the gloop below, the crowd let out a cheer.

Now Phil could concentrate on avoiding Stan. As his friend leapt from island to island, Frank realized Phil had a destination in mind. In moments, the Bayport Challenger was back at the island where he'd first tried to build a bridge.

"That plank is even shorter than the one he brought before," Joe said. "Unless he's got a hammer and nails on him, we've lost."

Phil glanced over his shoulder as his new plank clattered on the platform. Stan Dale was only two islands away.

Dropping to one knee, Phil retrieved the board he'd left on the island.

"Stan's almost on top of him," Callie hissed.

Phil swung the long board so it stretched from the corner of his island to the edge of the platform nearest to the safety zone.

Then Phil snatched up his second board. As he ran out on the new bridge, Stan landed on the island Phil had just vacated. The Champion was only a few steps behind.

Yet Phil stopped in the middle of his new bridge. Squatting down, he laid his second plank in place.

51

There was barely an inch on either side, but it reached the safety zone.

"That was the brainteaser," Frank breathed. "You needed to build a bridge on top of a bridge to get there!"

Phil hadn't reached safety yet. Stan dashed after him as Phil scuttled across his makeshift bridge. The frail connection flexed wildly as Stan put his weight on it. The Champion stabbed out a hand to grab the last feather just as Phil flung himself into the safe zone. Stan's hand clutched only air as he tumbled into the gloop.

Rune and Stan stood up to their knees in the stuff. The greenish brown gunk dripped in globs from their red uniforms. And over them, one feather still in his headband, Phil Cohen acknowledged the crowd's roar.

"It was nice of Phil to invite Stan to use the showers in our locker room," Joe said as they drove home.

Frank shrugged. "I guess space is limited in those trailers they're using."

"More likely, Stan wanted to avoid Rack and his big mouth." Joe frowned. "He was giving Rune a really hard time, and they're supposed to be buddies."

Although it was after midnight, traffic around the

arena was heavy. Joe swung away, cutting through the empty streets of Bayport's shopping district.

"Speaking of yelling," Frank said, "I told Fenner and Kayton my suspicions about the burglaries. They're going to check Artie Lake's background."

Joe shook his head. "For all we know, those burglaries could have been pulled by two different people."

"Looks like we might have a chance to find out," Frank said suddenly.

"How?" Joe demanded.

Frank simply pointed out the window.

They were passing Clifton's, the fanciest jewelry store in town. Frank had seen the store's white marble walls a million times. But this time something was different.

This time a black figure scrambled spiderlike across the carved stone!

6 Over the Edge

Joe's first reaction was to slam the brake pedal to the floor, bringing the van to a shrieking stop. Instead, he gently goosed the gas and the van moved smoothly onward.

Joe grinned. Why give the burglar any warning of detection?

Joe turned to Frank and pointed to the van's cellular phone. "Why don't you call the cops and report a B and E."

As Frank punched in the numbers, they were already past Clifton's brightly lit front. The store occupied the corner of Main and Cannon streets. It was considered a historic building, with its intricately carved facade. And right now, a burglar was

54

using that carving for hand- and footholds to break in. Clifton's next-door neighbor was a more modern office tower. It occupied the rest of the block, dwarfing the older building.

They reached the corner of the structure, and Joe sent the van into a tight turn. Frank had reached the police. He reported the crime-in-progress, adding details as Joe took the van around the block.

"Yes, that's right," Frank said into the phone. "He's entering Clifton's on Main. No, he was climbing down the carvings on the side of the building, on Cannon Street."

To Joe, it seemed as if the illumination hadn't been as bright on the side street. Maybe that was why the burglar struck there.

Whatever else you can say about this guy, he's got guts, Joe thought. Not to mention expensive taste, he added mentally. As he thought of the figure capering across the carvings, he realized this must be a real cat burglar. Funny that the media hadn't mentioned that.

As they made the turn onto Cannon Street, Joe killed the van's lights and cut off the engine. They silently rolled to a stop.

Yes, it was slightly darker here on the side street.

Joe scanned the roadway. He saw no broken glass on the sidewalk. A glance at the white building showed no one on the walls. But one of the windows on the top floor seemed slightly different from the others. It looked as if it was open just enough for someone to get in or out.

He turned to Frank with a grin. "I'd say our burglar is inside. What do you say we hang around to watch the cops pick him up?"

The police, however, had taken Frank's report all too seriously. At least three squad cars were heading for the store, each coming from a different direction. Joe could hear their sirens blaring from blocks away.

His face twisted into a scowl. "They're just going to scare our boy off. They probably expect a big car chase, too."

As he spoke, a masked face appeared in the off-kilter window. The burglar peered along the street and spotted the Hardys' van. Joe held still, but the burglar obviously realized there were passengers.

The figure stared for a long, hard second. Then the burglar jerked back from the window, disappearing into the darkness inside. In spite of the noise they were making, the police had not yet arrived.

Joe twisted the ignition key and revved the engine. "Looks like we'll have to do a bit more than just watch the show!"

He pulled back, then gunned the gas. The van jolted over the curb and onto the sidewalk. With a dexterous cut of the wheel, Joe pulled them up right against the wall. Above was the window where the burglar had appeared.

"Open your door," he said to Frank. "We can't get out on my side."

Frank flung his door open, and the two burst from the van. Joe turned right around, scrambling up the door and onto the van's roof.

"What do you think you're doing?" Frank stared wide-eyed up at him from the pavement.

"I'm going after that guy," Joe replied. "Since the door downstairs is probably locked, there's only one way in."

Frank came along behind, but Joe could hear him muttering. "For a guy who doesn't want to get involved in this case . . ."

Joe jumped upward, losing the rest of Frank's complaint. His hands caught the edge of the window that was partially ajar. Rough metal tore against his fingers. So that's it, he thought. The window had been pried open.

Tightening his grip, Joe pushed the window open a bit more. A new noise burst the air—the scream of a burglar alarm. Guess I got it to open, he thought, scrabbling for a hold.

Tucking in his legs, Joe rolled across the floor. He sprang up in a fighting crouch, in case the burglar was waiting to pounce. Joe spun around. But all he found was a large desk, some overstuffed chairs, a few filing cabinets, and a wall safe—unopened. The office appeared to be empty.

Joe caught the briefest flicker of movement in the doorway. It was a retreating black-clad leg.

He yelled out the window as he dashed for the door. "Frank, get up here! Now!"

Hurtling through the open doorway, Joe found himself in a dimly lit hall. Which way? The hall intersected two corridors. Joe chose the shorter distance.

He swung into the corridor just in time to see a door silently swing closed.

Frank's voice came from behind. "Where are you?"

"Here!" Joe yelled back. He dashed down the new hallway and yanked open the door. It had a sign marked FIRE STAIRS.

Joe held his breath, his heartbeat thudding in his ears. He could hear the clatter of footsteps in the stairwell.

"He's heading for the roof!" Joe called.

Joe charged upward, taking the stairs three at a time. He yanked himself along on the railing. Behind him, he heard the stairway vibrate as Frank joined in the pursuit.

The door to the roof was open. Joe darted through, half-expecting to be jumped. There was no attack, though.

Joe staggered to a halt, blinking his eyes. The roof itself was unlit. But there was a ghostly, reflected glow in the air. It came from the floodlights illuminating the building's walls.

Frank burst through the doorway. "Where is he?"

Joe wondered the same thing as he hunted around.

Then, over by the edge of the roof facing Cannon Street, he found his quarry.

Joe didn't get a good look. The burglar was just a blurred human form, a crouching figure silhouetted against the lights below.

The burglar alarm still gave off its deafening clang. Under that, Joe could hear the sirens of the police cars.

"Give it up!" he yelled over the uproar. "You can't get away."

The burglar-silhouette straightened against the glare. For an instant, it seemed to face off against Joe.

A second later, it jumped.

59

7 Incriminating Evidence

"*No!*"

Frank turned at Joe's horrified cry. He was just in time to see the burglar go over the roof's low parapet.

"I told him to stop—that he couldn't get away." Joe stared in shock. "Why did he take such a foolish risk? He couldn't possibly have survived the fall."

Frank ran to the spot, then turned back to his younger brother. "He didn't meet the fate you think."

Beckoning Joe over, Frank knelt and pointed to the cable fixed to the top of the store's ornate facade. Squinting into the darkness, he said, "The cable goes across the street. Looks like the other end is hooked to the top of a two-story building. When our friend jumped, he was probably hooking a pulley onto this for a fast getaway."

"That's the last time I waste any pity on this guy," Joe said gruffly. He kicked at the low wall. Then he hopped back with a cry of surprise. "Something's down there!"

Frank peered into the shadow cast by the parapet and saw the barest glint of metal. He reached down and came up with—a crossbow.

"Now we know how that cable got across the street," Joe said.

"We may know more than that." Holding the weapon out by its bowstring, Frank brought it into the light. "I can see the silver on this thing. But am I right that it was painted blue?"

Joe stared. "You're saying this is a team crossbow from 'Maximum Challenge'?"

Frank nodded. "I think the last time we saw this, it was in Callie's hands."

"Police—freeze!" a voice interrupted them.

The Hardys turned to find three police officers standing in the rooftop doorway. All had their guns out to cover Frank and Joe.

"Drop the weapon," an officer ordered.

Frank let the crossbow fall to the roof. "I think this may be a long night," he said.

"Raise your hands and keep them visible at all times!"

61

Frank and Joe kept quiet as they were handcuffed and marched downstairs. The lights were on in the office, where more police were gathering. Frank breathed a sigh of relief when he recognized the cop in charge. "Hi, Con."

Con Riley's eyebrows rose as he turned to see the Hardys. "Well, well," he said. "I thought the pair of you weren't getting involved."

"Excuse me, sir," one of the young patrolmen said. "These are the perps."

"We're not the perps," Frank said. "We're the ones who called you in."

"I figured as much," Con said. "And I'll bet you came in here to stop the real burglar." His face grew angry. "After certain people couldn't resist playing with their sirens."

The young officers looked embarrassed.

Con gestured for the Hardys to be released from their cuffs. "So what happened when you went after this guy?"

"He faked us out," Joe said.

"We thought we had him cornered. But he got away on a cable leading across the street," Frank reported. "I'm sure he's long gone by now."

Con sighed. "What a surprise."

"Nobody mentioned this guy was a cat burglar," Joe said.

"Don't breathe a word about that!" Con burst out. "You don't know how hard I've fought to keep those words out of the media. The last thing we need is a string of copycat crimes."

Frank looked at Riley. "Do you think these burglaries are the work of one person."

"They're very slick jobs," Con admitted. "I'd say lots of planning went into each score. Easy in, quick out."

"Sir!" Another young officer burst into the office. "We think we found how the perp got in. There's a rope leading down from the building next door."

"Easy in." Con nodded toward the unopened safe. "But it looks as though you interrupted our burglar before he got anything."

"And he left a clue getting out." Frank pointed to the crossbow carried by one of the other officers. "That comes from the set of 'Maximum Challenge.'"

Con's eyebrows rose again. "Does it, now?"

Frank nodded. "It might be worthwhile to check the backgrounds of the show's staff." He paused for a second. "Especially a guy named Artie Lake."

Joe looked like he was about to object, but Frank continued. He told the story about the bullet in the wrong place. "It could have been an accident. But combined with the crossbow . . ."

"It's not enough to hang this fellow, but it makes him worth looking into." Con picked up his notebook. "Let's get a full statement."

It was late before the Hardys got home. Frank

went through the whole next day only half-awake. He had to smile at the way everyone at school treated Phil Cohen. The victorious Challenger was Bayport High's new hero. The embarrassing news stories and the girls' defeat were forgotten. Everyone was talking about the Challengers' chances of beating the Champions.

Biff Hooper looked on silently as the whole cafeteria cheered for Phil. "You know, I could use some of that," he said. "The next game, I want a shot."

Frank arrived early at the arena that evening. He was surprised to find Biff already there. His big friend pulled him aside.

"This is my night!" Biff announced happily. "I was talking with that Artie guy at the door. He told me they're doing a strength test."

"I thought you were holding out for the stick-fighting with Rack or Rune," Frank said.

Biff gave him a sharp look. "Come on, Frank. Who's the strongest on our team?" He casually made a muscle.

Frank shrugged. "Okay, if that's the way you feel, big guy."

"It is." Biff grinned. "By the way, I found out the recipe for gloop. You mix lime Jell-O, blue food coloring, and baked beans for the lumpy parts."

"Yuck," Frank said. "Beans?"

Biff nodded. "And some chemical to keep it from going bad. Artie told me. He's a nice guy when you get to know him." He frowned. "But he seems worried about his job. His bosses and the cops have been asking a lot of questions."

And I'm the reason, Frank thought a little guiltily. Frank also had a reason for arriving early. He wanted to check with Harry, the prop guy, about a missing crossbow.

"How'd you hear about that?" The short man stared when he heard Frank's question. "It's weird. Last time I saw them was after we packed them up after the rock-climbing contest." Harry scratched his head. "The cops were around today, asking questions. Fenner and Kayton were pretty mad. They had to switch around some events, because they're short a bow. The cops want to hang on to it."

"Yeah, it's evidence," Frank said.

Not that he expected anything to be found on the bow. A burglar of the skill he'd seen wouldn't leave fingerprints.

They'll probably find Callie's prints, Frank thought. And maybe mine. He joined his teammates getting into their uniforms.

The evening's show was indeed a test of strength. Pat Serrone showed them the field of battle. Three scaffolding islands rose out of a lake of gloop. The middle platform held two big piles of foot-square concrete blocks. Half were painted red, half were blue. There was also a red and a blue island. Each was connected to the central structure by a swaying rope bridge.

"This is a straight race," Serrone explained. "Whoever moves all the blocks onto their island in the shortest time is the winner. Have you chosen your contender?"

"Right here," Biff said.

Frank was surprised when the Champions put up Eddie Millen. He was muscular, but a lot shorter than Biff.

"It's like my dad says," Biff said confidently. " 'A good little man can never beat a good *big* man.' "

Eddie grinned. "I prefer the one that goes, 'The bigger they come, the harder they fall.' "

"Gentlemen, take your places," Pat Serrone announced.

Eddie and Biff stood by the piled blocks.

"On your mark, get set . . . GO!"

Each contestant grabbed a block and set off across the swaying bridges. From the way they handled the cubes, it was clear they were pretty heavy. Biff did not have an easy time crossing the unsteady bridge. By the time he put his block down, Eddie was halfway back to the central island.

"Go, Biff!" The Bayport team shouted its support. Phil Cohen looked worried. "There's more to

66

this than physical strength. Crossing those bridges calls for balance."

"I see what you mean." Iola frowned. "A big guy like Biff is at a disadvantage."

Callie rolled her eyes. "Here we go again. The Champions have the experience. That's why they chose their *little* strong guy."

"Hold on," Joe said. "Give Biff a chance."

Slowly but steadily, however, Eddie pulled farther ahead. He ran, carried, and stacked, building a two-block lead. Soon he was four blocks ahead.

Biff began to get desperate. He snatched at his blocks. On his island, his stacks grew increasingly sloppy.

Eddie was down to his last ten blocks. Biff had fifteen. Puffing, he reached out and grabbed two blocks, carrying one under each arm.

"Way to go!" Callie yelled.

Frank wasn't so sure. The extra weight made the rope bridge droop and rock more wildly. Biff dumped his two blocks and raced back. Eddie still kept to single loads.

"BIFF, BIFF, BIFF!" the crowd in the stands was cheering.

Biff reached the middle island and loaded up again. He tried to run across the bridge. Instead, he ran into disaster.

Frank wasn't sure what happened. The bridge

might have twisted under the weight. Biff may have put his foot in the wrong place. Whatever the case, the rope and wood construction collapsed, and Biff was pitched over the rope safety rails.

A fountain of gloop rose into the air as he landed heavily.

Callie and Iola groaned; Joe and Phil sighed loudly.

Oh, well, Frank thought. At least Biff knows what he's falling into.

"I'm afraid Biff's fall disqualifies the Challengers," Pat Serrone announced. "This event goes to the Champions."

Eddie Millen dropped the block in his hands and raised his arms in victory. He still had seven blocks left on his island.

Rack was pumping his fist in the air. "Number One! Number One!" he chanted.

There were enough Rack and Rune fans in the house to pick up the cheer.

Frank wasn't listening. He stared worriedly out into the lake of gloop. Biff was just sitting up. He was moving very slowly.

"Do you think he hurt himself?" Iola's voice showed concern.

Frank and Joe headed to the rim of the tankful of gloop. But someone was there ahead of them. Artie Lake wore a pair of chest-high rubber fisherman's waders over his brown coveralls.

"I've got gloop duty tonight," Artie said. "I'll help him up." He climbed in and sloshed over. Biff had landed near one of the corners of his island. He winced and put a hand to his side as he tried to stand up in the sticky stuff.

Artie arrived, but Biff waved him off. Instead, he grabbed one of the steel poles supporting the platform above. He tried to pull himself up, making the scaffold shake.

On the island above, a stack of Biff's haphazardly placed cubes began to collapse. The falling blocks knocked against other stacks.

And suddenly, Biff and Artie were caught in an avalanche of tumbling concrete blocks!

8 Fists of Fury

"Oh, no!" Frank cried, but his voice was lost in the loud gasp from the audience. Pat Serrone calmed the crowd as crew members came running. Frank swung over and landed in the gloop. It felt unexpectedly cold as he waded toward the jumble of blue blocks.

Joe slopped after him. Farther back were Kendra Cassidy, Rune, and the stagehands. The boys only had to shift a few cubes before they helped a groaning Biff to his feet.

"I landed hard when I fell," he said. "Then one of those blocks clipped me." He cradled the right side of his chest. "Bruised some ribs, I think."

70

Leaving Biff standing quietly, the Hardys pitched in to help the Champions and crew people move a pile of blocks that had landed on Artie. He breathed noisily through his teeth, and every time he moved, he had to bite back an exclamation of pain.

"I really got creamed," the wiry stagehand said. "One of those blocks caught me hard on the shoulder, and it *hurts.*" Artie's face was pale under his shock of unruly hair.

Kendra tried to help him to his feet. She pulled gently on his arm. Artie gave a yelp of pain.

"This isn't going to work," Rune said. He wrapped his arms around Artie's chest and managed to haul him upright. But the stagehand's breath came in short, pained hisses.

"The gloop inside your waders is going to make it tough to walk," Kendra said. She gently tried to slip one of the shoulder straps off, but Artie flinched.

"He's got some broken bones," Rune announced. He turned to the other crew members. "See if you can get a stretcher. Otherwise, getting him out of this tank will be torture."

The stagehands returned in a few minutes with a canvas stretcher. Frank and Joe each took a handle as Kendra eased Artie aboard.

Four people slogged through the oozing glop, carrying the stretcher. Frank and Joe had one end,

71

while Rune and one of the stagehands handled the other. When they reached the edge of the tank, more helping hands were waiting outside.

Biff trailed along behind. The Hardys helped him over onto dry land. Hugh Fenner and Deborah Kayton joined the knot of concerned faces. "There goes our safety record," the producer muttered.

"Which is the best local hospital?" Kayton asked.

"Bayport General," Joe replied. "That's where we're taking Biff."

He glanced down at the stretcher, where Artie seemed to be resting comfortably. "Look, we've got a van. Give us a chance to get out of these clothes and we'll take Artie, too."

"We'd probably beat the ambulance," Frank called, halfway to the lockers.

The producer gave a quick nod and then he and the director huddled together as Pat Serrone continued to keep the audience calm and in their seats until Artie and Biff were taken care of.

In the locker room, Joe peeled off his sodden jumpsuit. "So this is gloop," he said, stepping around the growing puddle on the floor. "Yum."

"Let's hope that's the only time we have to play in it," Frank said.

In moments, the Hardys and Biff were in their street clothes. Joe took Biff along as he started up the van and backed it to the stage entrance. Frank came out, supervising four stagehands carrying Artie on the gloop-stained stretcher.

Frank and Artie got aboard, and Joe headed straight for the hospital.

When they reached the emergency room, the doctors and nurses were a little taken aback by Artie and his gloop-filled waders. Joe smiled as Frank explained what the greenish brown gunk was.

"So you *did* get the secret recipe," Joe teased as they waited for news from the staff.

A doctor came out to talk just as Hugh Fenner arrived at the hospital. "We can release Biff right now," the intern said. "His ribs are taped, but they're only bruised. The other gentleman has a broken clavicle."

"Ouch—a broken collarbone," Frank said with a grimace.

"And we'd like to keep him overnight," the doctor added.

"I want the best care for him," Fenner said. " 'Maximum Challenge' will pay for whatever his union insurance doesn't cover."

"I'm sure Mr. Lake will be glad to hear that," the doctor said.

Frank and Joe left Fenner to make the necessary arrangements. Then they drove Biff home. When they finally reached their own beds, they fell into exhausted sleep.

The next morning, Bayport High seemed like a funeral in progress.

"Well, we're back to being the underdogs," Joe said.

"Not only that, we've lost a team member." Frank nodded across the cafeteria. Biff Hooper sat stiffly in a chair. Several girls from the junior class had stopped to see how he was doing.

Joe snorted. "You'd think Biff was dying."

Frank cracked up. "Well, he's getting lots of attention—just not the kind he expected."

When the Bayport team arrived at the arena that evening, they found more bad news.

Joe got the first clue when he came in and saw the setup. The tank of gloop was still in place. But now a pair of ten-foot-tall cylinders rose out of the slimy stuff.

"Uh-oh," Joe muttered.

"Yup," a voice came from behind him. "It's dueling time."

Joe turned to find Rune sprawled in the stands, reading a book. Glancing at the cover, Joe gawked. The book was about new theories in physics. Frank had read it and found it hard to understand. Joe had gotten lost on page one.

Rune noticed Joe staring. "What? You're surprised that big, bad Rune can read?"

"No, it's just the subject matter."

74

The big man grinned. "I may be good at butting heads, but that doesn't mean I don't have a brain."

Joe pointed to the tall cylinders. "Are you going to be up there tonight?"

Rune shook his head. "Oh, no. That's Rack's specialty. He loves to push people around with his quarterstaff. I think he's watched too many Robin Hood movies."

"I thought you were Rack's friend," Joe said in surprise. "You don't sound like you are."

Rune shrugged. "Rack and I have been pals for years," he admitted. "We've been partners in more contests than I can count. But his head gets bigger and bigger every day. He talks about chucking the show and going into movies. Wants me to quit, too, so we can be partners. *The Adventures of Rack and Rune,* he'd call our first film."

The stuntman shook his head. "Rack has a guy working on a script. He's even talking action figures. He doesn't have an offer from anyone yet, but we're supposed to pack our bags."

"You don't want to go along?"

Rune twirled a finger along his mustache. "I know lots of guys who had TV hits. They thought they were big stars, so they left their regular shows. And nobody has heard of them since."

He gave Joe a lopsided grin. "Let's face it, kid. My 'talent' is for jumping around. Rack's talent is hitting people with a big stick."

75

Joe turned to stare at the setup. His teammates had all expected this challenge. Two competitors were to stand on the cylinders and duke it out with quarterstaffs. The six-foot sticks were padded at both ends for safety. And between the padding and the gloop, the ground below was a soft surface. But the fall from the small fighting platforms could bruise a person's pride.

Joe knew that all too well. He'd spent the last month as Biff's sparring partner. The big guy's dream had been to take on Rack at the quarterstaff. So Biff had set up a pair of oil drums in his backyard for practice. After the contestant search had been announced, Joe had found himself at Biff's almost every day.

They'd fought mock battle after mock battle. Joe had learned a lot about quarterstaffs—and a bit about bruises, too. The top of an oil drum didn't give much space to maneuver. Joe had quickly found that Biff's size and reach gave him a considerable advantage. He'd had to fight hard to give Biff a decent workout.

And after all that effort, their best stick-fighter couldn't play.

Biff groaned when he saw the two towers, and it wasn't because of his taped ribs. He'd turned up and put on his uniform, but he was not allowed to compete. The doctors at the hospital had been quite firm.

"Well, Joe, it's up to you," Biff said. Disappointment showed all over his face.

"I'll do my best," Joe promised.

Soon he stood high above the audience on top of the towering cylinder, a staff clenched in his hands. Across five feet of empty air, Rack leaned on his quarterstaff. The look on his face said, Easy win.

Over on dry land, Pat Serrone went over the rules—which were, essentially, that there were no rules. Joe tried to get himself ready. His fighting platform actually had a little more space than the oil drum he was used to, giving him some room to maneuver.

He heard the host's voice. "Ready—GO!"

Immediately, Rack jabbed at Joe's midsection, as if he were trying to poke Joe off his perch.

Joe turned sideways so the blow barely grazed him. But Rack's staff swooped around as if the stuntman were using it as a baseball bat. Joe blocked with his stick, forcing the padded rod down. For a second, Rack looked off balance. Joe rapped in with a quick blow to the shoulder.

Rack staggered back, surprised. But he recovered before he reached the edge of his tower. Behind the protective goggles of his helmet, the Champion's eyes squinted in anger. He walloped away at Joe, driving the Challenger to his knees.

But when Rack went for the final shove, Joe was

too quick for him. He got back to his feet and traded Rack blow for blow.

Maybe my sparring practice has paid off, Joe thought. Rack has about the same size and reach as Biff. And, Joe realized, there had been times when he'd even managed to knock Biff for a loop.

"Get him!" Iola's voice came over the crowd.

Joe leaned forward, trying to land a good one on Rack's head.

Rack ducked, his staff suddenly spinning. A jolt ran through Joe's body as the whirling stick caught him behind the knees. His legs folded, and he found himself sliding headfirst off the platform. All he could see was gloop.

No! Joe raged. He let the quarterstaff fall from his hands as he twisted in midair. He clawed at the top of his tower. For a second he caught hold, then nearly fell again as his body crashed into the cylinder.

Rack's staff thumped into Joe's back.

He's trying to jolt me off. Joe gritted his teeth and fought to strengthen his hold. Rack hit him again, this time pushing down. But the Champion couldn't get the right angle. Rack nearly toppled off his perch.

Joe couldn't see his opponent. He was too busy trying to shift around. If he could avoid Rack's thrusts and get the cylinder between them, maybe he could climb back up . . .

And then what? Joe asked himself. My staff is down there, sinking in the gloop.

He twisted slightly, finally getting a glimpse of Rack. The Champion looked even more furious than usual. To make matters worse, the audience wasn't cheering Rack on. Instead, the crowd was booing him.

Furious, Rack lunged, aiming for Joe's midsection. He's trying to knock the breath out of me, Joe realized—and knock me down.

Joe had an idea. He twisted away, then he swung back to catch the staff between his body and the cylinder. Maybe he could make Rack lose his weapon, too.

Rack tried to pry Joe loose with the trapped stick. The Champion tottered, losing his balance. But he clung to the quarterstaff.

Yeah, Rack, hold on, Joe gloated. This is what he was hoping would happen. Joe let go with one hand, and smashed down against the staff. It worked! Rack went over, screaming in rage.

Joe felt the fingers on his other hand give way. He slid down the cylinder.

But he had the satisfaction of seeing Rack hit the gloop first.

Joe splashed down and pushed up on his knees, grinning. By the rules of the bout, the first one to hit the gloop was the loser.

Rack heaved himself up blindly, his face and helmet goggles caked with crud. He pawed the stuff away until he could see Joe—and Joe could see the insane fury in his opponent's eyes.

Fists clenched over his head, Rack charged straight for Joe!

9 Trouble on the Line

"What's Rack doing?" Biff shouted as he watched the Champion charge Joe.

"He's gone berserk," Iola said, and gasped.

Frank was already in motion, bursting from the ranks of the Challengers. As he reached the wall holding back the gloop, he was joined by two figures in red.

"Rack, have you gone completely *crazy?*" Kendra Cassidy hissed. "We're on camera."

"For once, think before you swing," Rune said, rushing over. " 'Champion decks kid.' Is that the kind of publicity you want? Who'll build your action figures then?"

For a second, Rack loomed over Joe, his fists still shaking. Frank began climbing into the tank.

But the Champion suddenly turned away. Frank noticed that Rack used the move to kick more gloop onto Joe.

Rack climbed out of the tank to reach Pat Serrone and his microphone. "Okay, so you pulled even," the Champion said. "That will just make it all the sweeter when we beat you tomorrow!"

Challenger and Champion fans alike cheered from the stands.

Frank blinked. He hadn't quite realized that the Challengers had won this bout. But that meant the tiebreaker would be the grand finale—the big obstacle-course race.

"It will all come down to you, Frank," Biff said in the locker room as they changed out of their uniforms.

"Thanks a lot," Frank told him. "That makes me feel so much calmer."

As he and Frank drove home, Joe tried to lighten the mood. "This will be the first time in days we'll get to bed at a reasonable hour," he said. "No walking wounded to take to the hospital."

"No burglars to chase," Frank said with a grin. "We have been burning the midnight oil lately— and right when we're supposed to be in training."

Joe didn't laugh. "I wouldn't mind a little

burglar-hunting," he said. "Providing it let us nail Rack Rackham."

"You still think he's our cat burglar?" Frank asked in surprise.

"It could be anybody, from that quick glimpse we got," Joe admitted. "But Rack sure has the nerve for it. And I can always hope he'll be put away for six to ten years." He shrugged. "Anyway, he won't be doing anything tonight. Fenner has called a meeting of the whole Champions team. I heard he's going to chew them all out for losing their edge. Then he's going to go after Rack in particular for unsportsmanlike conduct."

Joe shook his head. "I'd say it was about time. At least it will keep Rack off the streets."

Frank stared out the van's windshield. "I don't think we're going to be bothered by any more burglaries."

Joe glanced over at his brother. "You don't?"

Frank nodded. "I don't think the burglar is up to it anymore. I had a chat with a doctor friend of Dad's at Bayport General. Artie Lake definitely has a broken collarbone, and they've got X rays to prove it."

"You've got Artie Lake on the brain," Joe said.

"Oh, yeah? And you aren't obsessed with Rack?" Frank inquired. "At least I can make up some sort of case against Artie. Artie as much as stuck a loaded gun in Iola's hands. The results could have been pretty bad."

Joe shook his head. "You can say what you like, but all you've got against Artie is a circumstantial case."

"So, I guess that crossbow we found on Clifton's roof flew there by itself?" Frank asked.

"No, somebody brought it there," Joe said. "Somebody involved with 'Maximum Challenge.' But that leaves us six team members and more stagehands than I've even counted. They all had the same chance to borrow that bow that Artie had."

Joe grinned. "And that could just as easily have been one Floyd Rackham. We're back at square one. But you shouldn't be worrying about the burglaries. You've got to get in condition for the big race tomorrow."

"Two days from now," Frank corrected. "Hugh Fenner wants to do it on a Saturday for maximum crowds. Besides, he's one stagehand short."

Frank sat back in his seat. "Anyway, we'll know who did it soon enough—when the burglaries stop. With a broken collarbone, Artie won't be swinging around on top of buildings." He began to look gloomy. "But it doesn't matter, because we can't prove it, anyway."

"You're beginning to act weird, bro," Joe said.

"I'm just facing facts," Frank responded. "The

police won't be able to catch Artie in the act if he's out of commission. The only way to nail him otherwise is by tracing some of the loot to him."

He suddenly sat upright. "Maybe there's more loot than we think. Working for a traveling show would be a great cover for a burglar. When we get home, I'm going to give Con Riley a call. It might be interesting to see if he's checked the other towns where 'Maximum Challenge' has taped. We can see if they've had their own little crime waves."

When they arrived home, Frank went straight to the telephone. Luckily, Con Riley was in the station house. He was a step ahead of Frank's brainstorm.

"Good thinking," the police officer told Frank. "I've already checked for suspicious burglaries along the show's back trail. That's the first thing I did when we found that crossbow. I picked up a list of locations from the producer and made inquiries of the various police forces."

"And?" Frank said.

"Our hunch was right," Riley responded. "Each town had a rash of burglaries while the show was taping the competitions. And they ended when the show people left."

"Do you have lists of what was taken?" Frank asked eagerly. "I'm sure you've been keeping an eye on Artie Lake. But with him hurt and out of circulation, he's not going to pull any more jobs.

The only other way to nail him is to trace the loot—Hurd Applegate's coins, the Bayview jewelry, stuff stolen in the other towns . . ."

"I've been getting faxes about the stolen items," Con interrupted. "Funny thing about this job. Do it for enough years and brilliant ideas like that become routine."

The sarcastic tone left his voice, and he sighed. "So far, we haven't found a trace around Artie Lake. I thought he might have pawned the loot from his last scores here in Bayport. That would be the easiest way for a traveling thief. He could dump the items he stole here at his next destination."

Con sounded frustrated. "But we've had no luck. Not one of our local pawnbrokers recognized Lake's picture. And nothing on the list of stolen goods has turned up."

"Well," Frank said unhappily, "it sounds as though you've done everything you can."

"Yeah." Con's voice was gruff. "Everything but catch this burglar." He paused for a moment. "I know Joe wants to keep out of this case. Officially, of course, that's how I feel, too. But I can't get anybody undercover at the arena. So if you come across anything at all, I want to hear about it."

"Of course, Con. You'll be the first to know." Frank hung up the phone, feeling worse than ever.

The cops are never going to pin this on Artie Lake, he thought. All he has to do is lie low until the show leaves town. He may even keep his loot stashed wherever it is and come back for it later.

Frank swallowed back a bitter taste in his mouth. As long as he doesn't call attention to himself, he's free and clear. He'll have outsmarted the cops . . . and he'll have outsmarted Joe and me, he thought.

The phone rang just as Frank was stepping out of the kitchen. He picked up the receiver. "Hello?"

"Frank Hardy?" a muffled voice came over the line.

"That's me. Who's calling?"

"No names. I've got a message for you, Hardy. Stop sticking your nose into the burglaries. You're beginning to annoy me."

Frank strained his ears, trying to catch a familiar note in the voice. The tone was tough and threatening. Did it sound like Artie Lake?

"And you don't want to get me annoyed. I left one bullet in that gun as a warning. But I've got lots more where that came from."

10 Leap into Danger

Joe headed for the kitchen in search of a snack. Instead, he found his brother shouting into the telephone. "Who is this?" Frank cried.

He looked up, shook his head, then furiously slammed the phone down.

"I can't believe you," Joe said. "Prank phone callers *look* for people they can annoy. Now they'll keep calling our number."

"I wish this joker *would* call back," Frank said. "He just told me to keep my nose out of the burglaries. Then he hung up."

"Hmmm," Joe said with a laugh. "Well, it wasn't me, although that's the way I feel."

"I was just thinking the smartest thing the burglar could do was lay low." Frank frowned in puzzlement. "Threatening me over the telephone isn't the best way to accomplish that."

Joe shrugged. "Maybe he's not as smart as you think."

"And why would Artie warn me against investigating if he can't pull any jobs for a while," Frank wondered aloud.

"Because, big bro, you were wrong about Artie all along." Joe beamed.

"For once, Joe, I think you may be right."

Joe couldn't get Frank's words out of his mind. He got up early the next morning and took a brisk run. On his way home, he stopped off at Con Riley's favorite coffee shop.

Joe had timed his arrival perfectly. Con was just finishing a hearty breakfast.

"Everywhere I turn lately, I'm seeing Hardys," the officer said, grinning. "Or hearing from them."

"Too bad you weren't listening in after you'd hung up last night," Joe replied. "Frank got a threatening phone call. Someone telling him to butt out of the burglaries. And they threatened physical harm."

Con's grin vanished. "Artie Lake? He was sent back to his hotel room with his neck in a brace and one arm in a sling."

"I don't think Frank's so sure about his prime suspect anymore," Joe said. "Which makes me wonder if you've gotten any info on the rest of the 'Maximum Challenge' bunch."

Con pushed his plate away and gave Joe a long look. "It might not be strictly according to regulations, but . . . come on."

The police officer led the way back to the station house. "I've been collecting information on the burglaries." Inside his small office, the desk was littered with papers.

"As I told Frank, we sent off a fax to the other towns 'Maximum Challenge' visited for tapings." Con tapped a sizable stack of paper. "Our burglar seems quite the one-man crime wave. We've circulated lists of stolen items."

Con pulled out some more faxes. "This is our background check on the show's staff. There are some reports of minor thefts on the set, Fenner has a number of parking violations, and two people have criminal records."

Joe eagerly scanned the sheets. Floyd Rackham had been arrested in several states over the years. Usually the charge was assault. Seeing Rack in action, Joe wasn't surprised.

The other arrest listed a two-year suspended sentence for breaking and entering. The defendant was a very young Ron Gruenwald.

Joe bit his lip. He was almost pleased to find out that Rack was dirty. But what about Rune? For the life of him, Joe couldn't square the husky guy who read physics books with the cat burglar he'd chased at Clifton's.

"Does that tell you anything?" Con's voice interrupted Joe's thoughts.

Joe remained silent for another moment, pretending to scan the faxes in his hand. He'd noticed something else on the desk. The piece of paper was turned away from him. But Joe had gotten pretty good at upside-down reading.

He made out the top line fairly easily. **PLANNED REDEPLOYMENT OF PATROLS TO HIGH-RISK BURGLARY AREAS** appeared in capital letters.

Joe quickly scanned the memo, trying to keep his face blank. This burglar has the whole force running around, he thought. But there is going to be a concentration in some places and almost no coverage in others. The memo said "high-risk burglary areas," but what that really meant was "high-rent." Joe could understand the plan. This burglar wasn't in town to steal bowling trophies. The stuff he wanted would be in rich people's homes.

Looking up from the faxes, Joe turned to Con. "I don't know what I can do with anything I've seen here." He smiled at the officer. "But I may get some ideas."

Joe spent a great day at school being hailed as the new hero. "I couldn't believe it! You tied the score," one of the guys from his math class said.

"Rack looked pretty angry when you beat him," a girl chimed in.

"It's just what he deserved," Iola said huffily. "That guy is a big bully."

"Yeah," Joe said with a grin. "I heard you yelling for his blood."

With his brother's new celebrity status, Frank didn't manage to get Joe alone until after supper.

"So what are we going to do with our free night?" Frank asked. "You want to turn in early? Or should we watch the tube?"

"I was thinking of going for a drive," Joe replied.

"Anywhere in particular?"

Joe nodded. "Yeah. Several places where we *won't* see any police cars tonight."

He explained about his visit with Con Riley and the memo he'd seen.

"The cops are basically putting more cars in rich sections, and where the burglar has been before. They're patrolling the mansion district—Hurd Applegate's neighborhood. And they have reinforcements in Bayview and in the downtown shopping area."

"Clifton's," Frank said.

"But they're taking cars away from areas they think are less likely to be hit."

"Like where?" Frank asked.

"Our neighborhood, for one. And the Harborside district is another," Joe replied.

"Well, there are a lot of new condos there, but most of that area is pretty grungy."

"With the cops covering the likely areas, I thought we might visit some long shots," Joe said. "Places where the cops won't be—"

"—that are possible targets for a burglar." Frank finished Joe's thought, and his eyes lit up with interest. "What do we know about our thief? He likes isolated locations. Applegate's place was in the middle of nowhere. And the houses in Bayview are pretty spread out."

"That's right. Nobody was around when he hit Clifton's," Joe said. "Now, what about the loot? I'd say our boy likes stuff that's valuable and *portable*."

"You've got a point," Frank said. "He got a coin collection and jewelry."

Joe pulled out a pad and a pencil. "So, what places are kind of deserted, full of something expensive and light, and short on cops?"

The boys came up with four or five possible sites. Getting into the van, they drove through town checking them out.

"This is a strong prospect," Joe said as he turned the van into the Harborside neighborhood. Brightly lit condominiums gleamed on some blocks. Other streets were full of shadows and grimy warehouses.

"Fulani Diamond Imports," Frank read off their list. He glanced around as the neighborhood became more shabby. "I never understood why Mr. Fulani keeps his office down here."

"His grandfather had this office, and so did his dad," Joe said. "Besides, he owns the building."

They pulled up across the street from an old, four-story brick building. The structure seemed to huddle beside a warehouse that was being turned into expensive apartments.

"Looks like the area is coming up in the world," Joe said.

"Maybe—but I'm not sure about the visitors."

A figure was coming down the dimly lit street. It threw an eerie shadow on the construction site.

Joe and Frank got out of their van. The figure froze for a second. Then the Hardys found themselves blinking in the beam of a strong flashlight.

"Frank and Joe Hardy!" the man behind the light cried.

Joe raised a hand to shield his eyes. "Mr. Fulani?"

Assam Fulani had had many dealings over the years with Fenton Hardy. He also knew Joe and Frank. The jewel merchant clicked off his light and walked toward the boys. His round, dark face looked a little pale.

"You gave me a scare," Fulani admitted. "What are you doing down here?"

"Keeping an eye out for burglars," Joe replied. "We heard the police were cutting patrols around here."

"I heard the same," Fulani said. "So I decided to check my place of business."

He glanced around the empty street, then at the two boys. "I would be happy for some company."

Frank and Joe followed the gem merchant to a thick metal door. Fulani poked a code on a keypad set in the door frame. "This temporarily inactivates the door alarm," he said.

Then the merchant dug a big key ring out of his pocket. After going through three locks, he pushed the door open.

As they stepped inside, Joe couldn't help comparing these surroundings with Clifton's. The jewelry store had the fanciest ground floor in town. This place looked more like a warehouse. But the two buildings were alike in one respect. Both housed a fortune in precious stones.

"First, let's check my office," Fulani said, starting up the wooden stairway. The little man moved with surprising speed. Joe felt a bit out of breath as they reached the third floor landing.

"Just through here," Fulani said, taking out his keys again. He undid three more locks, pushed the door open, and turned on the light.

The office was large, taking up the whole front part of the third floor. In one corner was a wooden desk and a worn leather desk chair. A low wooden table was flanked by ancient overstuffed armchairs.

The place looked as if it had seen better days, but it was comfortable. Joe glanced around, wondering where the safe was hidden. Every day, he knew, thousands upon thousands of dollars passed through here.

"I am a silly old man." Fulani chuckled away his fear. "Everything is as it should be."

"Not exactly," Frank said.

He was staring at one of the front windows. Actually, Frank was staring *through* it. Outside, poised on the window ledge, a black-clad figure stood frozen in the sudden light, a glass cutter in its hand.

The Hardys rushed for the window as the burglar flung himself away. Without thinking, Joe threw the sash open.

"The alarm!" Mr. Fulani cried.

But there was no screaming siren. "Aha," the gem merchant said. "He must have already disconnected it."

Joe leaned outside and spotted the burglar. "He's climbing a cable on that construction site next door."

Scrambling onto the window ledge, Joe glanced around. How had the guy gotten over there? he wondered. He must have jumped to that jutting girder. It was a healthy distance. But if the burglar could make it, Joe figured he could, too.

"Joe! Don't—" Frank began.

But Joe was already in motion. He dropped into a crouch and flung himself into the air. Ignoring the cries behind him, Joe sailed toward the girder in the distance.

Joe thrust his arms as far as they could go. His fingers touched the surface of the girder. He scrambled for a hold, but gravity worked against him.

He clung for a second, dangling. He could feel the cold metal at his fingertips, but couldn't get a decent grip. Joe was about to fall!

11 One Secret Revealed

For one brief second, Frank thought his brother was going to make it to the girder. Then Joe began to slip—and Frank could only watch helplessly.

Suddenly, Frank heard a loud clicking sound, and the burglar came hurtling downward. Frank realized the noise was from a rapidly spinning pulley. This guy must have a strong grip, he thought. Climbing up a pulley line meant holding onto *two* ropes at once. Otherwise, the climber went into free-fall, the unsecured side of the rope sliding through the pulley. Was that what had happened to the burglar? Had he lost his hold?

No! The black-clad figure pulled up beside Joe as if he were riding in an elevator. A slim arm shot out to catch the younger Hardy around the chest. Then the two of them swooped down to the open floor below.

The burglar dropped Joe off, then twisted away and swung to the sidewalk below. Before either of the brothers could shake off his astonishment, the burglar dashed away. In seconds, his black clothing had merged with the shadows. Then there were only rapidly fading footfalls on the pavement to mark his passage.

"Are you all right?" Frank called to his brother.

Joe leaned against an exposed I beam, his face pale, struggling to pull himself together. "I'll be back inside in a second," he shouted.

An instant later, Joe swept down on the pulley lines and dashed to the street-level door.

"Will he be able to get in?" Frank asked.

Mr. Fulani finally came out of his daze. "I can unlock from up here." He stepped to the desk and pushed a button on the control panel.

They heard a crash downstairs as the heavy door slammed shut. Then Joe came clattering up the steps, shouting, "Don't call the cops yet!"

Mr. Fulani froze in surprise, the receiver already at his ear.

Frank shrugged. "The burglar has disappeared by now. We may as well hear what Joe has to say."

A second later, Joe appeared in the office doorway. The run up the stairs had gotten his blood

99

going again. His face was flushed instead of the ghostly white it had been a few moments before.

Joe's blue eyes gleamed with a plan. "Am I too late?" he asked. "Have you already called them?"

"We have not yet informed the police," Mr. Fulani said.

"Good," Joe said. "I'd like to ask you a big favor. Would you mind not reporting this?"

Mr. Fulani's eyes seemed to pop out of his head. "My office is nearly broken into and you say I should *not* inform the police? Why?"

"Because if you call, the police will come. They'll probably blast their sirens, we'll have blinking lights outside, and they won't find anything. All they'll do is scare the burglar away." Joe shook his head. "That's what happened at Clifton's."

"If we don't call?" Frank asked.

"I'd say there's a good chance the burglar will come back." Joe smiled. "And we'll be waiting here as a welcoming committee."

He turned to the diamond merchant. "You see, Mr. Fulani, I have an idea. Can you think of a quiet way we can get back in here? Is there a side entrance or any way in besides the front door?"

"There are the fire doors downstairs." Fulani turned toward his desk controls. "I can deactivate the alarms, and you can prop open the doors."

He gave Joe a piercing glance. "Are you so sure the thief will come again?"

"This burglar likes to fake out the enemy. Twice, the thief has made a move, fallen back, and then made the exact same move. It's caught us off guard both times—but it won't again."

Frank opened his mouth to protest that they'd never seen any such thing.

But Joe raised his voice, continuing. "Moreover, the burglar will want to make sure no evidence was left behind. Like this." He held up his right hand, displaying the glass cutter.

"Where did you get that?" Frank demanded.

Joe shrugged. "I sort of swiped it during my swing for life." He turned to Fulani. "It's your choice, sir. You can call the cops and keep worrying about the burglar. Or you can go along with my idea and maybe end your worries tonight."

Frank stared at his brother through narrow eyes. Joe knew more than he was saying. But it was obvious he wasn't giving any more away in front of Mr. Fulani.

If you can't beat 'em, join 'em, Frank figured, and decided to go along with Joe's plan. "We'll relock the fire doors as soon as we're inside," Frank promised. "Look at it this way—you'll have a pair of free night watchmen for the evening."

Mr. Fulani glanced dubiously from one Hardy to the other. "You believe your brother is right?" he asked Frank.

101

Replying with a shrug, Frank said, "He's never steered me wrong."

But he's going to tell me *why* we're doing this as soon as we're alone, he silently promised himself.

Fulani's eyes went from the telephone to the window where they'd found the burglar. "So you think he will come back," the gem merchant muttered.

"Not if the police come," Joe said. "At least, not *tonight.*" He shook his head. "But after the police go, who can say?"

"After all, nothing was taken," Frank chimed in. "We're only asking you to put off your report till morning. If we don't catch the burglar, nothing has changed."

Assam Fulani's face twisted in thought as he assessed the greater risk to the precious stones in his vaults.

Finally, he gave an abrupt nod. "All right!" he said. "I won't report this now. You can stay here tonight. But"—he gave the Hardys a sharp look—"I'll be here at daybreak. And if you don't have the burglar, the police get called immediately."

Joe nodded. "Sounds fair to me."

Frank and Joe closed the window while Mr. Fulani pressed a few buttons on his control panel. "There!" the merchant said. "I have cut the fire doors out of the alarm circuit. You can prop the doors open without a problem. When you come back, just let them close behind you. Then, when you get up here, press this."

He pointed to a button on the panel. "This button will reactivate the alarms. And after that, whatever you do, don't leave! You'd set off a bigger racket than you'd ever imagine."

"That's all we need," Joe said. "Except your phone number—just in case we get lucky."

Fulani reached for his desk pad and scribbled off a number. "Now, if you're ready."

They turned the lights off, and Fulani left his office door ajar. Then they headed downstairs. Frank went to the end of the hallway to find the fire doors. He pressed gently against the panic bar and opened a door. It swung outward without a sound. Frank peered around quickly. The doors opened onto an alley behind the warehouse. He broke a piece of wood off a packing crate and slipped it so the door couldn't close. Then he rejoined Joe and Mr. Fulani at the front entrance.

They stepped out onto the street and waited as Fulani carefully reset the three locks. Then the Hardys got in their van, waving goodbye as Mr. Fulani headed for his car. In moments, they'd driven off.

Frank was behind the wheel this time. He went about five blocks toward home. Then he turned off, taking a roundabout route to the street closest to the alley behind Fulani's building.

They rolled to a stop on an even dimmer street than the one they'd left. Frank had killed the van's lights a good block before.

While Frank drove, Joe had rummaged around the van. "There are some things we might need," he said.

"Like a flashlight," Frank suggested. He glanced at his brother's back. "And what was all that stuff you told Fulani—"

"Oh, that," Joe interrupted. "Just a little creative convincing. Wait till we get inside. I'll explain."

They crept down the alleyway. Frank carried the reassuring weight of a five-cell flash in his hand. They didn't dare shine a light out here. It would give their presence away. But if need be, the metal flashlight would make a pretty good club. . . .

"Here's the door," Joe hissed. He pulled it open. Joe slipped in behind his brother. He kicked the makeshift doorstop away and stuck out his hand to catch the closing door. As the door swung shut, he eased it along. The click of the lock sounded very loud in his ears.

"We're in," Joe whispered.

"Let's just hope no one else came in while we were gone," Frank replied.

They crept through the blackness until they found the stairs. Then they ascended on tiptoe to the third floor. By the time they reached the office, their eyes had gotten used to the dark.

The door was still ajar. Frank let it swing a little wider and stepped inside. After the stairway and hall, Fulani's office seemed downright bright. The dim glow of a streetlamp came in through the front windows.

Still clutching the flashlight like a club, Frank peered around. No one was there.

He let go a breath he hadn't realized he'd been holding.

"Okay," he said. "Let's restore the security." He stepped over to the desk and pressed the button Mr. Fulani had indicated.

While Frank reactivated the alarms on the door, Joe came strolling in. He turned the armchairs so they faced the window and sat down. "Might as well be comfortable," he said.

"Listen, bro." Frank kept his voice to a whisper. But even so, his annoyance came through. "You know something you didn't know before you jumped through that window. Now give it up!" He glared at Joe. "And don't think you can fool me with nonsense the way you did with Mr. Fulani."

"Everything I said about the burglar's tactics is the truth," Joe said. "I saw it."

"And where was I when all that happened?"

"You were right beside me." Joe grinned at his brother's infuriated face.

"This case just gets screwier and screwier!" Frank complained. "The burglar sticks a live bullet in a gun that could have hurt anyone. He calls me up and makes threats. But when you get in trouble, he swings down and saves you. Why is that?"

"Easy," Joe said. "My burglar isn't your burglar."

Frank's jaw dropped. "What?"

"You said the person who called you up was a guy. But the person who saved me out there was a girl."

"How do you know—" Frank began.

Joe put up a hand. "I've hugged one or two girls in my life. I know what a girl looks like, Frank. That was a girl on that rope tonight. A thin girl, almost my height."

Frank frowned in the darkness. "A thin girl, almost your height, who dodges . . ."

"We saw her do it," Joe added.

"Both of us?"

But Frank could say no more. His brother, peering into the dimness outside, suddenly waved his hand. "Shh!"

Crouching low, Joe slid out of his seat and hid behind the chair. Frank followed his lead.

He couldn't believe what he was seeing. A black-clad figure swung across from the construction site and landed lightly on the windowsill. Then a gloved hand extracted a tool from a tool kit and set to work.

Seconds later, the window rose about six inches. The burglar swung around on the sill and squirmed through the entrance. Those moves would have been a tough job even for a trained acrobat, Joe thought. But somehow, this person made them look easy—and incredibly, graceful.

Joe waited till the burglar had taken a couple of steps into the room. Then he leapt from his hiding place, moving to block the window.

"Looking for this?" Joe asked, holding up the glass cutter.

Frank moved at the same instant, bringing up the flashlight. He shone it full in the burglar's face.

For a second, big gray eyes grew even bigger in the crude holes torn in the black silk mask. Then the burglar raised a slim, black-gloved hand to slide the mask off.

Curly red hair framed the burglar's face.

"I guess you've got me," Kendra Cassidy said.

12 The Final Brainteaser

Joe had expected a fight from Kendra. This, after all, was the woman who stood up to Rack Rackham in his bad moods. This was the burglar who'd coolly taken a dive off a five-story building to escape the Hardys. This was the person who'd risked her own life to swing him to safety on a dangerous rope.

He'd moved to block the Champion stuntwoman. But it seemed his effort wasn't necessary. Her shoulders had slumped the second Frank's light hit her. There seemed no fight in her at all.

Kendra shook out her hair, an odd half smile on her lips. "It's over now," she said. "It's out of my hands."

Frank lowered his flashlight slightly. "It sounds as if you're almost glad to be caught," he said.

"Glad," Kendra echoed. "That's for sure. It's like the end of a long nightmare."

"Except you're going to wake up in jail," Joe said. He pointed to one of the armchairs. "Why don't you sit down? I guess we can put the lights on now, Frank."

Frank went to the wall switch as Kendra sank into the chair.

"Why do you do it?" Frank stared at the girl as if she were some sort of strange science specimen. "It can't be the money. You don't pull down as much as Rack and Rune, but you must be making good bucks."

"Money?" Kendra laughed bitterly. "I'm raking in more now than I could have dreamed of two years ago."

"So what is it?" Joe asked. "Do you do it for fun? Does it give you a thrill?"

Kendra's only answer was a shudder.

"And where does your accomplice fit in?" Frank demanded. "That was more than a prank phone call when he threatened me. He knew too much. But he must have known I suspected Artie Lake. What was going on? Or was it just someone you got to call?"

"Call?" The word seemed to spark something in Kendra's face. The hopeless look disappeared. She glared at Frank with burning eyes. "You mean he called you? You actually *talked* to him?"

"Yup. He got on the phone and threatened me." Frank was torn between anger and bewilderment. "I imagine you know who it was."

"I just *wish* I knew!" Pain showed in Kendra's eyes. "For the last two TV seasons, I've wished and wondered."

She leaned back in her chair, glancing from Frank to Joe. Both of the Hardys were staring at her. "You asked if I pulled these jobs for money or for kicks. The answer to both questions is no. I'm not greedy, and I'm not crazy."

Kendra put her face in her hands. "But I am being blackmailed."

"Blackmailed?" Frank said blankly.

"What did you—" Then Joe realized what he was saying, and he stopped.

Kendra looked up. "What did I do?" A ghost of a smile came to her face when she saw Joe's embarrassment. "Oh, it's not a big scandal. The supermarket tabloids wouldn't make a big deal out of it."

She shrank into herself again. "It would just land me in jail for a few years."

Joe's eyebrows went up and he shot a look at Frank.

"You see," Kendra went on, "I didn't need any on-the-job training to become a cat burglar. I'd done it before I got on 'Maximum Challenge.'"

Silence filled the room. Frank and Joe didn't know what to say.

Kendra sighed. "Let's go back a couple of years. When I was in high school, I was good in sports. Hey, I was better than a lot of guys on the school teams. And what did that get me? A gymnastics scholarship to a college I couldn't afford."

She shifted in her chair, as if trying to shrug away the past. "What was I going to do? I knew I was sort of cute and I had the fighting spirit. So I went to Hollywood. If I didn't make it as an actress, I could always work as a stunt person, I figured."

"But it didn't work out that way," Joe said gently.

Kendra nodded. "There were lots of girls who were better-looking than I. And I quickly discovered you have to get into a union to do stunts. My money was running out, and I couldn't even get a job as a waitress."

She stared at the floor. "I was two months behind on my rent and hadn't eaten for a week. Then I decided I'd use my talents to get even. I was starving, but you couldn't imagine the money I saw being thrown around! Agents and producers who were turning me down had fancy homes, filled with all kinds of expensive toys. I told myself I would just take my fair share."

"What about alarms and other security devices?" Frank asked.

"I had always been good with tools," Kendra

replied. "And I picked up a lot from my dad—he used to install burglar alarms." Her lips tightened. "He'd probably be shocked if he found out how I've used what he taught me."

"So you became the Beverly Hills Cat Burglar," Joe said.

"More like Malibu and the Canyons." Kendra shrank under the Hardys' gaze. "It's not like I was a one-woman crime wave. When I really needed money, I'd—do a job."

"So what happened," Frank asked.

"Believe it or not, I got my big break. One of the female Champions got injured. They auditioned for a replacement, and I got the job." She shook her head. "All of a sudden, I had steady paychecks coming in. Big ones, too. I got myself a better place to live—though I spend most of my time on the road."

She looked down again. "And I sent out some anonymous checks—payback for things I'd taken. I know it sounds silly, but I kept a list of people I stole from. My idea was that I'd pay them back when my career took off." Her voice got tight. "Then the notes came."

"Notes?" Frank said.

"They'd appear in my dressing room, in my trailer, sometimes in my hotel room. They had to be from somebody connected with the show." Kendra looked up. "They knew about me. They knew the pawnshop where I fenced my loot. They had proof that would land me in the slammer."

"And they—he—wanted money," Frank said.

"That's the weird thing." Kendra ran a hand through her hair. "The blackmailer wanted me to go back to burglary. Every time we'd come to a new town, I'd get a list of places to hit."

"So you've been doing this for two years?" Joe asked in disbelief.

Kendra laughed, almost hysterically. "The funniest thing is, I'm getting offers to leave the show. This agent—one of the first guys I robbed—now thinks he can make me a star. He's lining up some film roles for me. Real films, not like the stuff Rack is trying to peddle. After all, action heroes like Rack are a dime a dozen. But a female action hero like me—"

She broke off. "I can't do it. The blackmailer won't let me leave. I've turned down several offers. The agent thinks I'm playing hardball, holding out for better parts."

Kendra choked. Was she laughing again? No, Frank realized. She was crying. "If they only knew!"

Frank and Joe looked at each other over the weeping girl's head.

This would be easy enough if we were cops, Joe thought. We'd just put her away and turn the show upside down to find the blackmailer.

But Joe wasn't a cop, and it was cases like this that made him doubt he'd ever be one. He'd thought they'd be clearing up the whole case when he set up his trap. Instead, they'd caught a new victim and faced a deeper mystery.

From the look on his brother's face, Joe could see that Frank didn't know what to do either.

Obviously, what they had to do was get a line on the brains behind Bayport's burglary wave. "You don't know anything about this blackmailer?" Joe pressed.

"I've never even *seen* the guy, much less talked to him. It's like dealing with a ghost." Kendra turned her tearful gaze toward Joe. "Or, rather, like being haunted by one. I arrive in town. It seems like ten minutes after I'm assigned a dressing room, there's a note waiting for me."

She shuddered. "That's the hit list for the new location. There are addresses, sometimes even maps, and, of course, what I'm supposed to steal. By the middle of the week, another note magically appears. That one tells me where to leave the loot."

Frank's eyes lit up. "Have you already been told where to drop off tonight's haul?"

The young woman nodded. "It's going into the set for tomorrow's race."

"The obstacle course?" Joe asked in disbelief.

"That's right," Kendra replied. "I've got an exact place to leave it."

Frank leaned forward, frowning in concentration. "And you got that in the middle of the week? How many people on the show know what the set will look like at that point?"

"I—I wouldn't know," Kendra said slowly. She glanced at Frank in admiration. "I hadn't thought of that."

"Join the club," Frank said. "Joe and I haven't been thinking much this week either. We first linked the burglaries and the show as sort of a joke. Even when we got serious, we kept zeroing in on the physical side of the burglaries."

Joe nodded. "So our suspects were Champions or stagehands." He grinned. "I was really hoping you'd turn out to be Rack."

For the first time, Kendra's laugh sounded natural. "A lot of people on the set would cheer if you could put him away."

"But the fact of the matter is, there was a division of labor here." Frank's eyes were far away as he pulled his thoughts together. "Kendra did the dirty work, but somebody else did the dirty thinking."

"That's a nice way of putting it," Joe said.

"Since it was Kendra who actually pulled the jobs, Artie is back to being a suspect," Frank pointed out.

"It can't be Artie," Kendra broke in. "The notes began appearing a show or two before Artie was hired."

"I knew it wasn't him!" Joe said. "But who could it be?"

Frank was onto something. "What we need is a guy who knew our phone number—and knew about the bullet in the prop gun. He also had to know about my suspicions of Artie Lake—but not know that Artie got hurt in that accident."

Frank's smile got bigger and bigger. "And when you put all this together, there's only one guy who fits the bill!"

13 A Different Kind of Crime

Joe gave his brother's face a keen glance. "Are you trying to say you know who the blackmailer is?"

Frank nodded. "We knew it had to be somebody from the set because of the special knowledge he or she seemed to have," he said. "We forgot one important thing. The blackmailer also had some special ignorance."

"Ignorance?" Joe and Kendra both echoed.

"Think about what the blackmailer didn't know. When I got that threatening phone call, the guy on the other end didn't know about Artie Lake's accident. There's only one 'Maximum Challenge' staffer who wasn't there to see those boxes fall. I'll give you a hint—he was in Boston at the time."

Kendra's mouth fell open and her eyes grew wide. "Chuck Purvis?"

"*Chuck Purvis?*" Joe's voice was a lot louder and more disbelieving. "I never liked the guy. He always seemed like a real Hollywood phony to me."

Frank grinned and raised his eyebrows. "Not to mention the fact that he tripped you in front of the news cameras."

Joe felt his face getting red. "Yeah," he said gruffly. "I'd prefer you didn't mention it." But he looked steadily at his brother. "I think you're sticking your neck out by accusing him of being the mastermind behind Kendra. *Especially* since you only have that one clue."

"I think I've got more than that," Frank said. "You didn't like my circumstantial case against Artie Lake. But I realize I can make a stronger case against Purvis."

He leaned forward. "Think back to when we were kidding with Artie Lake. Who was around when you suggested that 'Maximum Challenge' and the burglaries were connected?"

Joe frowned as he searched his memory. "Nobody was around," he said. "We were coming in the stage door, and Artie was on guard."

"Think again," Frank pressed. "We came in. Artie teased us about being detectives, we joked back, then took a couple of steps. What happened then?"

"Actors," Joe said. "You said something about actors." The memory came back. "You made a crack about actors to Hugh Fenner."

"And who else was with him?" Frank went on eagerly.

Joe closed his eyes, visualizing the scene. "Deborah Kayton . . . and Chuck Purvis."

"So, Purvis was around to hear about our interest in the burglaries. He's the one who found out we solve mysteries, too. Remember his tone of voice when he talked about it with Fenner?"

Joe shrugged. "I thought he sounded kind of annoyed with himself. He hadn't connected our names as contestants with the stories he'd seen in the papers."

"That's what I thought at the time," Frank said. "Looking back, I think he was nervous."

"You might be pushing it," Joe warned. "But I have to admit he was there to hear our run-in with Artie. How do you explain the bullet in the gun?"

"From the beginning, I had a problem with that," Frank said. "If the bullet was meant to hurt one of us—well, it wasn't aimed very well."

"Aimed?" Joe gave Frank a look of puzzlement.

"I'll put it a different way," Frank said. "Suppose we hadn't noticed the bullet. What would have happened?"

Frank turned to Kendra, who shrugged. "Pat Serrone would have been shooting off the gun to

119

distract the contestants. He's done it hundreds of times."

Frank nodded. "He wouldn't point the gun at anybody, would he?"

"No," Kendra said. "He shoots it up in the air."

"So the bullet would have wound up in the ceiling. Maybe it would hit one of the television lights." He turned to Joe. "But how would it get to us?"

Joe shook his head. "I don't see where you're going with this."

"I'm saying the bullet only makes sense as a threat to us."

"Well, it was," Joe said. "When Iola picked up the gun, any of us could have gotten hurt."

Frank smiled excitedly. "That's right, but maybe we should turn your sentence around a bit. Any of us could have gotten hurt *if* Iola picked up the gun."

"You're losing me, Frank." Joe noticed Kendra's baffled expression. "In fact, you're losing *us.*"

"It's still a question of aim." Frank spread his hands, trying to get the others to see his point. "We were only in danger if one of us picked up that gun. How could whoever planted the bullet know we'd do that?"

Joe and Kendra were both silent for a moment. "He—" Joe began. "Um . . . it . . . There's no way he could have been sure."

120

"Not if he wanted to hurt us. But I don't think that was the idea. I think the bullet was meant as a warning. Or maybe it was supposed to distract us, to keep our attention on the show instead of the burglaries."

A picture popped up in Joe's memory. "You said it could have been a warning." He frowned. "And you said it didn't make sense, because it depended on us finding the bullet."

Frank gave Joe an encouraging smile. "But it does make sense if someone came along to draw our attention to the gun."

"Nobody did that," Joe objected. "Unless you count Artie Lake rushing up with that box."

"But somebody *did* come along," Frank pointed out. "He started talking about the gun and found he didn't need to call our attention to the bullets. We'd found the live round already."

Joe fell silent again as the memories played out in his mind. He'd been putting the revolver back in the box. Then someone had come over to scold him about fooling with the prop gun. And who had it been? Chuck Purvis!

"You're right," Joe admitted. "He took the gun to Hugh Fenner."

"That's what he said he was going to do," Frank cut in. "I wonder if he really intended to go that far. Purvis looked pretty annoyed when I went with him to complain to Fenner. He may have only meant

121

to come over, get us to notice the real bullet, and then whisk the gun away."

Joe gave in. "Okay, okay, you've made your case. Only it's as strong as the case you made against Artie Lake, and we know he's innocent."

"I think it's stronger," Frank said, "especially when you consider the threats over the phone and Purvis's position as advance man."

"All right, I'm convinced." Joe frowned. "The problem is, we've got to convince the cops. And all we've got is a lot of what-ifs and maybes." He grinned. "Our most solid evidence is that Purvis looked annoyed."

"So we've got to dig a little more," Frank said.

"Too bad Purvis didn't show up dirty on the police background check. That would have been a start."

"Where does he come from, anyway," Frank asked.

"California, like Rune," Kendra said. "In fact, they knew each other when they were kids. I think Rune was the one who got Purvis the job on the show."

Joe whipped around. "Purvis and Rune were friends as kids?"

Rune, he thought. The only one on the show who had a record—a conviction for breaking and entering. A burglary that happened when he was young.

Joe headed for the door. "We've got to get out of here," he announced. "Let's go to Rune's hotel. I've got some questions for him."

"Whoa," Frank said. "We *can't* go out. Remember? I reactivated the alarms. If we open the doors now, we'll have the cops all over us—not to mention Mr. Fulani."

Joe stopped in his tracks. "Oh, right." Disgustedly, he dropped into a chair. There were things they should be doing, people they ought to see. Instead, they'd be stuck here all night. And how would they explain Kendra's presence when Mr. Fulani showed up at dawn?

Of course, we could let her go before he arrives, he thought. We can just send her out the window. . . .

Joe nearly erupted from his chair. *Out the window!*

"Hey, Frank," he said. "Suppose we leave without disturbing the doors?"

"How do you expect to do that?" Frank began. Then he followed Joe's gaze to the open window. "Oh," he said. "Oh, no. Not that way. The last time you took that exit, you nearly broke your neck."

"That's right," Kendra said. "I nearly had a heart attack when I saw you try that jump. Whatever made you take such a stupid risk?"

Joe stared. "Well, *you* did it."

"I certainly did not!" the stuntwoman replied. "I swung over on the pulley ropes."

"Do you still have the ropes secured out there?" Joe asked.

"Of course," Kendra said.

Joe turned to Frank and grinned. "As I said, why don't we leave through the window?"

Frank gave in. "We'll have to do it in shifts," he said. "I'm not trying a triple-decker Tarzan swing on that rope." He glanced at Kendra.

"We can go two at a time," she said. "Joe and I will go together. Then I'll swing back to get you, Frank." She looked down. "That way, you don't have to worry about me . . . uh, disappearing."

"We weren't worried about that," Joe said.

"You shouldn't be," Kendra said. "This guy has made my life a nightmare for two years. I want to see him nailed."

"There's one more thing," Frank said.

Kendra turned to see what new conditions Frank was going to make.

"On the way out, could you reattach the burglar alarm on the window?" Frank grinned. "We don't want anyone breaking in here while we're gone."

The swing from the window was one of the wildest rides Joe ever took. Kendra made him stand on the edge of the window ledge, holding the ropes.

"Hold them tight," Kendra said. Then the stuntwoman vaulted onto Joe's shoulders and grabbed the ropes, too. "On your mark . . . get set . . . GO!"

Joe felt like something out of a circus trapeze act. He pushed off from the ledge, gripping the pair of ropes tightly in his hand. The air rushed past him with a *swoosh* as he swung across the front of the Fulani building. The construction site zoomed at him.

"Let go!" Kendra called.

Joe released the ropes and dropped to a concrete floor. He was moving faster than he expected and tumbled when he landed. But he rolled and was on his feet as Kendra slid down the rope for a perfect landing.

"Now I'll go back to get Frank." She readjusted her hold and backed up a couple of steps. Then she swung back over to the window ledge.

We gave her the right name, Joe thought. As a burglar, she's graceful as a cat.

Frank joined Kendra on the ledge. He closed the window, and she fiddled with some wiring on the window frame. Then the two of them swung over and landed easily.

"Do we know where Rune is staying?" Joe asked.

"He's in the same hotel as I am," Kendra replied.

* * *

Ron "Rune" Gruenwald answered his hotel room door on the second knock. He wore pajamas and carried the physics book Joe had seen him reading earlier.

Rune looked a little surprised to see his midnight visitors. "What's going on?"

"We have a couple of questions for you," Joe said. "About Chuck Purvis."

"Chuckie?" Rune's face reddened. "That's what we used to call him when we were kids. Don't tell him I said that."

"Actually, that's what we want to hear about," Frank said. "The days when you were in school together."

"We weren't that close," Rune said. "We used to hang in the same crowd. A kind of tough crowd, really, in a town outside of L.A. I got into some trouble with the law. Chuck was the only one of us who went to college."

Rune chuckled. "He worked his way through school as a clerk in a pawnshop. It was a real dump—shady, too. I heard the owner acted as a fence, buying stolen property from all sorts of crooks."

"What—" Kendra's voice cracked. "What was the name of the pawnshop?"

"Fulbright's. It was right on the main drag in town—"

"I know the place," she said, glancing at Frank and Joe. "I used to use it myself."

"So maybe you knew Chuck," Rune said. "Although I'm sure you wouldn't recognize him from his college days. He had long hair and a beard, and wore these goofy glasses. . . ."

Kendra's face went pale as she heard the description. "I never paid much attention to him," she said hoarsely.

But it looks like he paid attention to you, Joe thought. "Well, thanks," he said out loud. "You've been a big help."

"What's going on?" Rune said. "Is Chuck in some kind of trouble?"

"We can't tell you what's going on right now," Frank said. "But we'd appreciate it if you could keep our visit here quiet."

Rune shrugged. "Why not? I marked Chuck down as an ex-friend years ago."

The Hardys followed Kendra to her room. As soon as the door was closed, Joe turned to Kendra. "Sounds like you remembered Chuck."

She ran a hand over her face. "He looked like such a creep. Who'd have thought he'd do so well?"

"That's not the problem," Frank said. "We've managed to clinch our circumstantial case. But we have nothing concrete to connect Chuck Purvis to the burglaries."

"Unless we catch him with the loot." Joe smiled slowly. "Which means we need some more loot for him."

He turned to the other two. "What do you say we burglarize Fulani Imports?"

14 Jumping the Gun

Frank looked at his brother in horror. "Are you out of your mind?" he demanded.

He stared as Joe stepped over to the hotel room's telephone. "Oh, I think we can keep this burglary legal."

Joe reached into his pocket and pulled out a crumpled piece of paper. "I brought Mr. Fulani's home phone number. First, I'll call him for permission."

He picked up the receiver, then stopped, glancing at Kendra. "I'm afraid we'll also have to call the police, too."

Kendra sat on the edge of her bed. Her slim form huddled in on itself. "It was nice while it lasted,

129

guys." She gave them a wan smile. "But you're right. It's time for me to turn myself in."

Joe punched in the phone number and waited for a moment. "Mr. Fulani, it's Joe Hardy," Joe said into the receiver. "No, no, everything is fine. I've got good news for you. Half of the burglary ring we're up against has given itself up." Joe smiled at Kendra.

"Yes, sir, that's right, it's a ring. And yes, only half."

Joe paused for a second, and Frank could hear excited chattering coming from the phone. "Yes, we want to get all of them, too, Mr. Fulani. That's why we want to talk with you and the burglar. I think you should hear her story."

Another pause. "Yes, *her* story. No, I haven't called the police yet. I have another favor to ask."

Joe's grin grew larger as he explained what he had in mind. There was a moment of silence on the line, then Frank heard Mr. Fulani's voice again.

"Does my brother think it's a good idea?" Joe glanced at Frank, his eyes twinkling. "Mr. Fulani, it *is* his idea."

Joe listened for another moment, made his good-byes, and hung up. "Fulani will meet us in twenty minutes," he announced. "I guess we'd better rush back to the store."

It finally hit Frank. Joe had never mentioned

where he was while he talked with the gem merchant.

"Come on, come on!" Joe ushered them out of the room. "It would be embarrassing if Mr. Fulani caught us outside his building."

"What about the police?" Kendra asked in a dazed voice.

"We'll call them after we're comfortably seated in the office." Joe gave them both his most reassuring smile.

Frank found himself feeling glad the streets of Harborside were empty. For the third time that night, Kendra Cassidy and the Flying Hardy Brothers swung to the window of Mr. Fulani's office.

Kendra went first, disabling the alarm and opening the window. Then she pitched the rope to Joe. He swung over as if he did this every day. Then it was Frank's turn. He took the rope, remembering Kendra's words of advice: "Don't look down!"

Frank didn't. He saw nothing except a blur of passing bricks as he whizzed through the air. Landing on the window ledge was tricky, but he'd had a little practice by now.

He threw the rope back toward the construction site. As he was closing the window, a car's headlights lit the street below.

"Here comes Mr. Fulani," Frank announced.

Joe was already on the phone, speaking to the

police operator. Kendra sat in one of the armchairs. Her hands were clenched together.

Frank heard the downstairs door open. Then came the sound of Mr. Fulani's shoes on the stairway. Joe was hanging up as the gem merchant came in the door.

"The police will be here in minutes," Joe announced. "But first, I'd like you to hear this young lady's story."

Fulani came in clearly prepared not to like Kendra. That's understandable, Frank thought. I wouldn't be thrilled with anyone trying to steal my jewels.

But as Kendra told her story, Fulani became more sympathetic.

"Blackmail, you say?" The merchant shook his head. "What a dirty business."

By the time Kendra was finished, Fulani was willing to go along with Joe's scheme.

"I will even try to convince the police," he said. "This is a good plan, young Frank."

Joe's smile faded a little when he heard that.

Frank grinned. He realized Joe had forgotten he had credited Frank with the plan to get Mr. Fulani on board.

The police arrived, led by Officer Riley. Con was willing at least to listen to the Hardys. Frank was pleasantly surprised when Riley thought their plan might work.

Perhaps the police officer felt some sympathy for Kendra. Certainly, he appreciated her willing confession and wholehearted desire to help. And when even Fulani agreed to go along with the fictional burglary, Riley was convinced.

Con took it on himself to wake up Chief Collig. When he finished on the phone, he glanced at the Hardys. "The chief says it's a go," Riley announced.

"Excellent!" Fulani said, coming into the office. "Here's the bait." He had a large suede pouch in his hand. When he tossed it onto the desk, it landed with an impressive clank.

"What's in there?" Con asked.

Fulani shrugged. "Odds and ends. Some broken hardware items, bits of copper pipe, and an old doorknob."

"Well, it will look good, hidden on that set tonight," Con said, and turned to Frank, Joe, and Kendra. "I've gotten all your statements, so I guess you're free to go." He glanced at Kendra. "I wouldn't go too far, though."

She nodded in mute agreement.

The boys left by way of the alley exit. Kendra went with them, clutching the suede pouch. They got into the van, dropped Kendra at her hotel, and finally went home. The sun was just rising as they tumbled into bed.

Frank slept late that morning. This wasn't a

school day, and he planned to take it easy. Better save my energy for the grand finale, he thought.

Frank had a general idea of what he'd be facing that evening. The two teams would gather at opposite ends of an elaborate obstacle course. One Challenger and one Champion would be picked as runners. They'd race through the course in opposite directions. The members of the opposing team would do their best to keep the enemy runner from getting through.

"I'll think about it later," Frank muttered, yawning. He padded down to the kitchen. Joe was sitting in front of the remains of a hearty breakfast. He had a copy of the *Bayport Times* spread in his hands. A big grin threatened to split his face.

"Awful news, Frank," he said. "That cat burglar has struck again. Just about looted Fulani's, it says here. And the poor police don't have a clue."

Joe turned the paper so Frank could see the screaming headlines.

"Nice job," Frank commented, scanning the story. "If I didn't know better, I'd almost believe it."

Joe got a bit more serious. "Let's hope Chuck Purvis believes it. Until we link him to the burglaries, Kendra will be taking the heat alone."

Frank felt just as concerned. "So if Purvis takes a walk, Kendra will take the fall." He brightened a little. "On the other hand, we've built this up as the

134

biggest haul she's ever taken. I think we can depend on Purvis's greed."

Joe nodded. "Kendra will plant the loot right before the finale tonight. As soon as we finish in there, the cops will close in. They'll stake out the set and seal the arena so tight that a bug won't be able to get in or out without being noticed."

"They'll nail him," Frank said. "I'm sure of it."

I only wish I felt as sure of *my* chances, he thought nervously.

Evening finally arrived. Before he and Joe left for the arena, Frank put in a call to Con Riley.

"Everything's set," the police officer assured him. "You may notice a few more blue uniforms this evening, but they're mainly there for crowd control. Nothing is going to happen until Purvis arrives, and he's been delayed flying out of Boston. Bad thunderstorms. Run that race quickly, and you may be done before he even arrives."

Frank and Joe drove to the arena, and battled what seemed like a record crowd. A crew member they didn't know opened the stage door. The Hardys reached the locker room to find Biff and Phil already there. Their teammates were playing a loud game of basketball using a wadded-up paper towel and a trash can.

"Two points!" Phil's voice echoed off the tiled walls.

Frank shook his head. These guys are wound up pretty tight, he thought.

There was a lot of laughter and horseplay as they put on their uniforms. But Frank could feel the tension underneath. Each of his friends asked him at least once how he was feeling.

They left the locker room and met the girls.

"Hey, guys," Iola greeted them. "How's it going, Frank?"

"How's it going?" Frank realized his voice was too loud. "It's going great! Hey, everybody, here's a team announcement. Everything's great and I'm feeling fine."

"You don't have to bite my head off," Iola complained.

Frank took a deep breath. "Guys, I'm sorry. It's just that I'm beginning to feel like a prize pig at the state fair. Everybody's asking how I feel. I guess the real answer is—I'm scared."

Joe glanced at his teammates. "I guess we're all feeling the pressure."

"Yeah," Biff said. "This is the tiebreaker. Oops." He put his hand over his mouth. "I guess I'm not making it any easier."

Frank had to laugh. "Anyway, I promise to do my best. And if I made any of you mad, I hope you take it out on the Champions."

The Challengers cheered. "Excellent pep talk, dude," Joe said with a grin.

As they walked through the halls to the arena, Biff and Phil began chanting, "Number One! Number One!"

"Knock it off, you two," Callie said. "Rack will probably think you're cheering for him."

The entire arena floor had been turned into a sea of gloop. Islands of scaffolding arose from the mucky stuff. Some of them were small. Some were large, broken up with tall wooden walls. There were planks and rope bridges, tightropes and pipes just big enough to crawl through. Frank spotted metal chutes, catwalks, stairways, and rope ladders. And in the middle was a bridge that looked more like a seesaw.

"Tons of fun," Frank muttered. To get through all this, he'd have to run, jump, climb, crawl, and slither.

And, he thought, I'm getting a chance to check it out beforehand. That probably means they're going to make the competition worse. I wonder how.

He found out as Pat Serrone lined both teams up. Frank would be up against Rune as the runner. The two of them received helmets and goggles. The other team members were all presented with high-powered water guns.

"You've all done great so far," the host said. "But now we go to sudden death. If either runner lands in the gloop, he loses. If either is hit by these water guns, he loses." Serrone smiled. "And we'll know if you're hit. The guns are full of concentrated grape juice."

He turned to the other team members. "Snipers should watch where they're shooting. If you squirt your own runner, your team loses!"

Pat then pointed to the far sides of the obstacle course. "Each starting area is marked by your team flag. The first runner to reach the other team's flag is the winner. Champions, Challengers . . . take your places!"

The two teams trotted to the flags that matched their uniform colors.

"Are you ready?" Serrone asked.

Rune waved. Frank nodded.

"Then . . . *go!*"

Frank set off at a dead run. He left the starting island and crossed a thin board to reach the first obstacle. It wasn't too tough—a wall that was nearly nine feet tall. Frank bent his knees slightly, then ran and leapt. His fingers grabbed the top of the wall—and the whole thing began to pivot!

Great, he thought. They didn't mention that this maze was set up like a carnival fun house.

Frank rode the wall to the other side of the island and rolled off. He dashed across a rope bridge this time. The next island had several walls, a ladder, and a couple of walkways. Which was the quickest way through? he wondered.

I'll climb the lowest-level wall—it looks the most direct, Frank decided.

But as he scrambled atop the wall, he found a nasty surprise. There was a big hole in the floor beyond, with gloop glistening below.

If I'd hopped over without looking, I'd have landed right in that stuff. Frank's eyes narrowed. Even now, it looked too far to jump.

A sharp *splat!* made him look down. The wall he was straddling suddenly had a big purple stain a few inches from his foot.

Frank glanced up. The Champions were spreading out, moving ahead through the islands. Janine Harris had just gotten in range. She had nearly eliminated him before he'd barely begun.

Frank saw another figure in red taking aim. He swung back over the wall, hiding behind it as he heard the splatting sound again. He turned to the rope ladder dangling behind the wall. It led to two metal walkways. One seemed to cut across the island he was on. The higher one connected to the next island in line.

Frank decided to take the high road. As he climbed up the rope, he saw one of his teammates running toward the wall.

"Watch out," he called out. "Big hole below!"

"Fine with me," Biff responded. "I just need a good place to shoot from."

With Biff laying down covering fire, Frank reached the catwalk with little trouble. Not only did it provide a bridge, it gave him an aerial view. He spotted several hidden traps as he ran along.

Even better, he thought, I'm above squirt-range up here—

His thought was interrupted as a stream of grape juice sprayed up through the metal trelliswork.

"What?" Frank gasped. He stared around wildly to find one of the Champions perched precariously on top of a wall three islands away, trying to spray him.

Another squirt came toward him, and Frank flung himself back. He fell to the openwork metal floor of the bridge. He could see straight down a good twenty-five feet.

That's when he noticed the figure in brown on the island below. Frank frowned. What was a stagehand doing in the maze during the show? The guy wasn't carrying tools. He wore a baseball cap with the bill hiding his face, and he slunk along as if he knew he didn't belong there.

Grape juice flew past Frank's face, dripping down. It pattered on the plywood below, and the intruder glanced up.

Frank's stomach tightened. This guy definitely didn't belong here.

Chuck Purvis had come to collect his loot early!

15 The Maximum Challenge

"What's he doing here now?" Frank demanded through clenched teeth.

Frank figured Purvis had come straight from the airport. In the brown crew outfit, he'd probably strolled in through the stage door unnoticed. And if he'd spotted extra police around, well, maybe that had pushed him into a hasty move.

As these thoughts raced through Frank's mind, he backpedaled down the bridge. His sudden retreat threw off the aim of the Champion sniping at him. He reached the rope and slid down behind the cover of a wall.

I have a lot more than the game to worry about now, Frank thought, frantically scanning the audi-

141

ence. No one seemed to notice the out-of-place stagehand—especially the cops. If Purvis finds that phony loot, he'll make his escape before I can warn anybody. And Kendra will face burglary charges alone.

Frank landed on a little platform—probably designed to be a sniper station. From there, he surveyed the obstacle course. Most of the action was going on at the higher levels. That probably made for more spectacular camera angles, Frank figured.

Chuck Purvis must have known that, too. He was taking the floor-level tour of the course. His route would take him slowly but surely—and unnoticed —to the drop-off point, which was one island from the midpoint of the course, marked by the seesaw bridge.

It was up to Frank to cut Purvis off. He hoped he could get help along the way. Frank turned back to the rope he'd just gotten off. It was knotted, meant for climbing. But he saw he could swing on it as well. It was a little risky, but with luck he'd drop onto a chute that led to the next island. Equally important, it led downward.

Taking a deep breath, Frank held tight and kicked off from the platform. He swung around the front of the wall. Then he loosened his grip, sliding down the rope but still controlling his fall. His surprise appearance let him drop to the chute without anyone shooting at him.

He was whipped down the metal surface, yelling at the top of his lungs, "Joe, Kendra—Purvis is here!"

Almost too late, he realized the slide was going to drop him in the gloop. Frank grabbed a metal pipe that helped make up the framework of the island. He almost strained his shoulder, but he managed to fling himself to safety.

There was a bridge down at this level, made of colorful plastic pipe. Frank dove inside, hearing the splat of grape juice on the plastic. He crawled as fast as he could, arriving on the next island to a barrage of Champion fire.

Frank didn't even try to evade the shots. Maybe that's why they missed. The Champions expected him to zigzag. Instead, Frank ran straight out. Purvis was only two islands ahead.

The only way forward, however, was by a long rope. Here's where I lose the game, Frank thought. He leapt up to grab the cable. Swinging hand over hand, he reached his destination miraculously unstained.

Up in the stands, the crowd was going wild. The noise didn't help as Frank pointed and tried to shout. Callie peered down at him from a catwalk overhead. "What are you saying?" she yelled down. "What's on purpose?"

"Not *purpose*," Frank called back. "It's Purvis! Tell Joe that Purvis is here. *PURVIS.*"

His scream came in the middle of a momentary lull in the roar. One person in the arena heard Frank and understood.

Unfortunately that person was Chuck Purvis.

The blackmailer whirled on the rope ladder he was climbing. He glared at Frank for a second, then began climbing faster.

Frank faced another pipe bridge. If he crawled through that, Purvis would only pull farther ahead.

Instead of going into the pipe, Frank leapt on top. It wasn't easy to run on the pipe's rounded surface. But he moved more quickly than by crawling through it.

Frank's insistence on taking the low road was drawing the Champions downward to take potshots at him. Some Challenger teammates were also moving to offer cover.

"I see Rune!" Joe's voice cried in a lull in the cheering.

"What about Purvis?" Frank thought the blackmailer was just ahead of him on this large island. But the way walls cut the place up, he couldn't see the guy.

All of a sudden, Frank couldn't see anything. A spray of grape juice hit him right in the face. It spattered his goggles, covered his nose, and even went in his mouth. Frank doubled, up, choking.

Overhead, Kendra Cassidy shouted, "Gotcha!"

Frank's voice was hoarse and raspy as he looked

up blindly. "Kendra, Chuck Purvis is here! He's going for the loot, and he's already reached the far end of this island."

Somehow, he made himself heard over the cheers and boos coming from the crowd. As Frank wiped grape juice off his goggles, he saw Kendra whip around, scouting.

Over the loudspeakers, Pat Serrone announced Frank's elimination. Frank ignored the host, moving to follow Kendra and intercept Purvis.

"Frank!" Serrone's echoing voice filled the arena. "You've been hit. The game's over."

Frank scrambled to the top of a wall and spotted Purvis. The blackmailer was halfway across a plank bridge leading to the island where the loot was stashed.

Waving one arm wildly, Frank pointed with the other one. He nearly fell off the top of the wall. But at last, Serrone noticed. His reverberating voice exclaimed, "What's that man doing there? All Security to the obstacle course!"

Which way would Chuck Purvis jump? Would he panic and run? Or would his greed force him to grab the loot?

Frank sighed in relief as Purvis went for the loot. It hung from the underside of the island's lowest floor. But members of both teams were now beginning to converge. As Purvis fumbled around under the platform, he suddenly jerked upright. A huge grape juice stain dribbled down the back of his brown uniform.

Frank glanced up to see Kendra Cassidy charging along a metal catwalk.

Well, Frank thought, that's marked Purvis, and good. As long as he's in those coveralls, he can't deny he was here.

But the clinching evidence was the suede bag of phony jewels. Purvis had to be caught red-handed with it. If he opened the bag to find it full of junk, he'd ditch it. Frank could only hope the TV cameras were catching Purvis's actions.

From his vantage point, Frank could see that Purvis had snagged the bag. Purvis rose to his feet, only to be struck by two streams of juice. Now Kendra and Joe were uniting their fire.

Rune arrived on the island. He ran onto a catwalk above Purvis, stared, and started clambering down.

Joe and Kendra opened fire again.

The blackmailer glared up at them with hatred on his face. His hand slipped into his coveralls.

He's got a gun, Frank suddenly realized. Purvis was so near and yet so far. Ten feet of air and gloop separated the two of them.

Frank saw a ladder with wooden rungs tied to ropes leading to the level above him. It would have to do.

He grabbed one of the rungs, ran back, then dashed for the edge of his island. Out, out, out he swung. Frank was more than halfway between the islands now, flying above Chuck Purvis.

The blackmailer had drawn a gun half out from under the brown jumpsuit.

Frank let go of the ladder. He tumbled down, crashing into Purvis. The gun clattered to the platform floor. But Purvis clung to the bag of loot as they grappled.

The blackmailer tried to shove Frank away. Frank only fought to cling to Purvis. They rolled, coming close to the edge. Then they fell into the gloop.

Both teams and a host of security people gathered to haul Frank and Purvis out. Frank turned to one of the policemen he recognized.

"Officer Waldner!" he said. "I want you to witness what this man has in his hand."

"What?" Purvis stared at the pouch he still held. He began to toss it into the gloop, but a powerful hand seized his wrist. The pouch fell to the platform.

"What's going on, Chuckie?" Rune still held Purvis's wrist.

"Payback time!" Purvis spat. "You guys get big bucks to clown around with these stunts. But I get zilch. I set up the arenas. I get the contestants. I should be the director—even the producer. But no, I'm just some lousy flunky. And you expect me to be grateful to you for getting me the job."

Purvis jerked his head at Kendra. "When she

came on the show, I saw my chance. She used to steal stuff and pawn it at my uncle Mortie's shop. So I figured she could do it for me."

The blackmailer smiled in evil triumph. "It was a sweet setup. I went from town to town, just doing my job. But I also did advance work for *her* jobs. Then I'd pick up the loot and drop it off with Uncle Mortie. Yeah, it was sweet—until those two got in the way!"

He glared at the Hardys. "Kendra barely pulled two jobs and they started saying the show must be involved. So I tried to set up a mystery to distract them."

"The bullet," Frank said.

"Yeah," Purvis rasped. "I figured you'd go after the Champions—Rack or Rune. But no, you had to go to Fenner and start talking burglars." He turned to Kendra. "And *she* had to lose one of the show's crossbows."

Rune dumped the contents of the suede bag onto the platform. One glance at the worthless junk, and Purvis lunged for Kendra. Surrounding police officers pounced on him as he screamed, "You set me up! You lousy—you set me up!"

"Sounds remarkably like a confession to me." Frank watched as the cops dragged the raving Purvis away.

"And on camera, too," Joe said.

"Between that performance and her testimony,

Kendra has a chance of getting off lightly." Frank smiled.

"With the way Hollywood is these days, she'll probably become the subject of a TV movie."

"Well, I've had enough of TV," Frank said. "But I'm sorry about losing the race."

"Guess we'll just have to make do with some wonderful parting gifts." Joe began to laugh.

"I don't think that's so funny," Frank said.

"It's not that. It's you!" Joe glanced at Frank and began laughing even louder.

Frank looked down. From head to toes, he was dripping gloop. "You've worn this stuff," he complained. "Why is it so funny to see it on me?"

"Ever since I learned the secret recipe, I've been waiting for a chance to say this." Joe was holding his sides with laughter.

"Say what?" Frank sighed.

"Frank's in beans."

THE HARDY BOYS® SERIES By Franklin W. Dixon

**LOOK FOR
AN EXCITING NEW
HARDY BOYS MYSTERY
COMING FROM
MINSTREL® BOOKS
EVERY OTHER**

Can superpowers be super-cool?

the secret world of

ALEX MACK™

Meet Alex Mack. It's her first day of junior high and
everything goes wrong! Until an accident leaves her
with special powers. . .powers that can be hard to
control. It's exciting. . .and a little scary!

ALEX, YOU'RE GLOWING!

BET YOU CAN'T!

by Diana G. Gallagher

A new title every other month!

Based on the hit series from Nickelodeon®

 A MINSTREL BOOK

Published by Pocket Books

1052-03